Five Stages of Grief
After the Alien Invasion

CAROLINE M. YOACHIM

Denial

Ellie huddled in the corner of her daughter's room. She sang a quiet lullaby and cradled her swaddled infant in her arms. Lexi was four months old, or maybe thirteen months? Ellie shook her head. There hadn't been a birthday party, and thirteen-month-olds didn't need swaddling. She tried to rearrange the swaddling blankets so they didn't cover Lexi's face, but every time she moved the blankets, all she saw underneath was another layer of blankets.

"Oskar?" she called. "Come and hold the baby for a bit, I need to go out and buy formula."

Oskar came in and gave her the same sad look he'd worn all week. Work, she decided, must be going poorly. She wished he would confide in her about it, but he didn't like to burden her with his problems. Lexi's room was dark, and the light switch wasn't working. Ellie opened the blinds, but the window was covered in white paint, making it impossible to see outside.

"Did you paint the windows?" she asked. Their apartment was on the third floor, and it had a lovely view of the treetops. "Lexi will want to see the birds."

"Sporefall killed all the birds," Oskar said, his voice bitter, "and we don't need formula. It's been months, Ellie. I know how hard this is, but I can't do this anymore. The pain is bad enough without reliving it with you every day."

Ellie frowned. "If you're too busy to watch the baby you should say so."

1

Oskar leaned down and kissed the top of her head. "I'm going, Ellie. There's a caravan heading down to L.A., and I haven't heard a thing from Jessica since sporefall. She didn't even answer the letter I sent about Lexi. I've hired a caretaker to help you get by without me, her name is Marybeth. She lost her wife to the sporefall, so maybe you two can help each other get through your grief."

"A little extra help around the house will be nice," Ellie said. "Tell your sister hello."

Ellie smiled. Jessica was a good influence on Oskar. She'd cheer him right up.

Oskar's eyes were teary when he turned to leave the room. She wondered if his allergies were acting up. He'd said something about spores. When she went to get the formula, she could pick up an antihistamine for him.

Ellie put Lexi in the high chair, still swaddled in blankets, and tried to spoon-feed her pureed peas. It wasn't working very well. Four months was too early for solids and the entire jar ended up on the blankets rather than in the baby. Ellie put the empty jar in the sink.

Someone knocked on the door, unlocked it, and came inside. It wasn't Oskar.

"Your husband gave me a key," the woman said, "I'm Marybeth. You must be Ellie."

Ellie nodded, "And this is Lexi. She's a bit of a mess right now." Ellie dabbed at the blankets with a napkin, then added, embarrassed, "She's a bit young for it, but I tried to feed her."

Marybeth smiled sadly. "Lexi died, Ellie. Nine months ago the Eridani seeded the planet with spores. Once they realized the planet was inhabited, they undid the damage as best they could, but they came too late for the elderly and the very young."

"Well, I'm glad they came nine months ago and not now," Ellie said, wiping the tray of the highchair with the food-smeared napkin. "Oskar hired you to watch Lexi? Do you do laundry, too? Her blankets are a mess."

Marybeth carefully unwound Lexi's outermost blanket and put it in the laundry hamper. "It would be better if you could move on, Ellie. This isn't healthy."

Satisfied that Marybeth could take care of Lexi, Ellie went to the bathroom and took a shower. Cold water poured down around her skin, and she scrubbed until she was red to be sure she got rid of all the spores. Oskar was allergic to spores, and she didn't want to make his

CLARKESWORLD
AUGUST 2014 - ISSUE 95

FICTION

NON-FICTION

Neil Clarke: Publisher/Editor-in-Chief
Sean Wallace: Editor
Kate Baker: Non-Fiction Editor/Podcast Director
Gardner Dozois: Reprint Editor

Clarkesworld Magazine (ISSN: 1937-7843) • Issue 95 • August 2014

symptoms any worse. Oh, but the babysitter—she came from outside, she must have been covered in spores.

Ellie ran out from the bathroom, dripping wet and wrapped in a towel. "You came from outside! You've exposed poor Lexi to spores!"

Marybeth put one hand on Ellie's shoulder and gently guided her back to the bathroom. "Hush now, the spores are gone, all grown into plants. We don't have to worry about spores."

Marybeth returned the next day with an old man. Ellie hoped he wasn't sick. He was dressed too warmly for the weather: clunky black boots, several layers of baggy clothes, and a fleece hat with flaps that covered his ears. He was short and stout with ashen skin and a grin too broad for his face. It made him look like a toad, Ellie thought, then pushed the uncharitable thought from her head.

"Come in, come in," Ellie said, then realized that her welcome was too late and Marybeth and her—was the man her father? Maybe her grandfather—were already in the entryway of her apartment.

"I thought it'd be good for you to meet one of the Eridani," Marybeth said. "It might help you come to grips with what happened."

"Nice to meet you, Mr. Eridani," Ellie said. It was time for Lexi's nap. The apartment was warm, good for sleeping, but Ellie could use some fresh air. "Do you sing, Marybeth?"

"Sing?" Marybeth asked. "No, not really."

"What about you, Mr. Eridani?" Ellie turned to the old man. "Will you sing my daughter lullabies? I'd like to go for a walk."

"It might be good for her to get out of the house," Marybeth told her grandfather. "I think Oskar made a mistake in painting the windows." She went over to the kitchen window and pried it open, sending flecks of dried paint flying everywhere.

Ellie turned her back on the kitchen, trying to protect Lexi from the nasty paint dust. "Don't let her breathe the dust, she just got over a terrible cough."

The old man nodded, then held out his arms to take Lexi. He held her gently, and while his mouth was fixed in the same broad smile, his bulging black eyes seemed sad. Ellie wondered if he was longing for grandchildren of his own.

"Don't be sad. Lexi clearly likes you. She didn't even cry." Ellie put on a sweater and opened her apartment door. "I won't be gone long."

The trees along the edge of the sidewalk had oddly purple leaves, and the people that passed looked far too weary for a sunny Saturday afternoon, but as she walked beneath the open windows of her apartment,

3

she could hear the low hum of a lullaby, slow and sweet, sure to soothe her daughter straight to sleep.

Anger

Amelia was twelve the night the spores fell, and she remembered it vividly. Thousands of meteors burned bright as they fell through the atmosphere. Charred black pods burst open when they crashed to the ground. By dawn, the air was filled with swirling clouds of orange mist, like pollen blowing from the trees. Every person and creature on the planet breathed the spores. The birds were the first to die, but not the last.

"Come away from the window, Sis." Brayden tried to tousle her hair like she was six years old or something. "Dad will be home soon, and you haven't done your homework yet."

"I didn't do my homework because it's stupid to pretend that nothing has changed," Amelia said. "Everyone in my class lost people to the spore. Friends, grandparents . . . siblings. Tia's parents got killed in the riots. Zach's older brother died in one of the fires. Then the way they healed us—"

She shuddered. She still had nightmares about the croaker that thinned into some kind of fog and poured itself down her throat, picking the spores out of her lungs and healing the damage the sprouting plants had done. It was that or die when the spores grew, but she'd still thrashed so much that Dad had to hold her down to keep her from hurting herself.

"It was eleven months ago," Brayden said. He stared at the sky for a moment, lost in his own thoughts. "What's the alternative to going back to normal? If you didn't have school, you'd sit home and sulk all day like that guy that came down from Portland."

Their neighbor's brother had showed up on the caravan last week, looking for Jessica, but she'd already left for the space station. She was one of the scientists chosen to help negotiate a treaty with the aliens. The only treaty Amelia wanted to see was 'get off our planet and take your damned purple plants with you.'

"Oskar sits around and sulks all day," Amelia said, "but I would go out and kill croakers."

Brayden shook his head. "You can't kill croakers. People have tried. They can't be poisoned, stabbed, or shot. No matter what you do to them, they recohere, they heal. If you did more of your homework, you might know that."

4

Unlike the rest of her classes, which she'd given up on, Amelia had paid careful attention to all the details of croaker biology. Despite their solid-seeming forms, croakers were essentially sentient fog. The squat froglike body they used on Earth was a dense gray cloud, thick enough to hold up the clothes they wore, but little else. Projectiles and blades passed right through and did little harm, and poison passed through unabsorbed.

Amelia had a different plan. She would trap a croaker bit by bit in a hundred glass jars. Then she'd throw the jars into a fire, one by one. Would the pain of that death be as bad as the last desperate gasps of her little brother? Gavin was four, and screamed all his last night in pain and fear. Spores made his lungs burn, the doctor said.

Amelia would make a croaker burn.

Croakers wandered the streets like ghosts, occasionally stopping to eat leaves from the purple plants that had grown from the spores. According to the news, the croakers were observing, collecting data so they could repair more of the damage they did at sporefall, but as near as Amelia could tell, the big gray frogs were just making themselves right at home. Amelia waited behind one of their licorice-smelling plants with a cardboard box full of glass jars.

A croaker came to nibble at the leaves, and she jumped out from behind the bush, jar in hand. She scooped out a big section of the croaker's ugly frogface. The croaker was thicker than she expected, like gelatin or pudding, rather than air. The gray goo in the jar was repulsively flesh-like, and her stomach churned as she screwed the lid into place. The croaker let out a high pitched whine. Its face appeared unchanged, despite her jarful of gray goo.

She couldn't do it. She had a boxful of jars, and she wanted the croaker to burn, but she couldn't bring herself to take another scoop of its ashen flesh. It stared at her with round black eyes, still making a high pitched sound, though softer now, a sad keening sound.

"You killed Gavin!" she screamed. "You messed up my whole world and now you stay here like you own it! You should burn for it!"

She hurled the jar of gray goo at the sidewalk. It shattered against the concrete and shards of glass flew everywhere. A cloud of gray swirled up from the shimmering fragments of the jar before drifting back onto the croaker. Into the croaker.

She grabbed another jar from her box and threw it at the croaker. It bounced off the alien's face, and the froglike grin didn't even flinch. "Go back to where you came from!" she shouted and flung jar after jar at the croaker, until her cardboard box was empty and the sidewalk was buried beneath a pile of shattered glass.

The croaker scooped up the broken glass in big webbed hands, mounding it and sculpting it into its own image. Amelia watched, fascinated despite herself. The croaker smoothed the bits of glass as easily as a sculptor might shape clay. It made a statue of a croaker, and in the statue's broad glass hands there was a human child with indistinct features. Not her brother, but a child like him. Perhaps all children like him. Unlike every croaker Amelia had ever seen, there was no froglike grin on the statue's face.

Brayden ran over. "I heard all the noise, and—" He stared at the statue.

"I wanted to set a croaker on fire, but I couldn't do it." Amelia said. "Not even after everything they did."

Perhaps it was a trick of the light, but the statue didn't look empty. Delicate orange flames danced inside the statue of the croaker, complete with thin wisps of gray smoke that reminded her of the swirling cloud when she broke the jar and let the croaker go. It had left a piece of itself inside the statue, to burn inside the glass.

She thought her mind was playing tricks on her, but Brayden saw it too. "They already burn for what they did."

The croaker bowed its head, then turned and walked away.

Bargaining

The alien standing in front of Jessica was four feet tall, slate gray, and shaped like an oversized toad. It smelled like chalk and made a quiet wheezing noise, barely audible over the hum of the orbital stabilizers. The temperature onboard the station was comfortable for humans, but the alien wore a thick sweater, knitted by one of Jessica's former graduate students as a gesture of goodwill from all humankind. A large round button with the number 17 was pinned to the purple wool. Eridani didn't use names.

Eridani 17 extended a webbed hand. The flesh of its fingers thinned, creating the illusion of wisps of smoke curling up from its palm. The smoke shaped itself into North America, and then a city skyline.

"Toronto?" Jessica asked. The city had a distinctive tower. Eridani 17 shook its head.

Negotiating with the Eridani was like a game of Pictionary, except that Jessica was sober and—thank god—didn't have to actually draw anything. Her brother Oskar had always been the artist in the family, excelling at Pictionary even when he was half her age. If his most recent message was any indication, all he ever drew now was pictures of his estranged wife, who lost her mind after sporefall killed their baby.

"Seattle," Jessica said.

The Eridani understood spoken language, but not by translating individual words. According to the best available translation, the Eridani heard ideas in the spaces between the words.

She hoped that this was true. She was not authorized to ask for what she truly wanted, and the sessions were recorded.

Eridani 17 transformed its speaking hand into an image of several Eridani standing between two skyscrapers. As Jessica watched, a giant web appeared between the two buildings, soon followed by several pods filled with what she guessed were baby Eridani.

"Seattle has a substantial human population, but I'm sure we can find an abandoned region that suits your needs," Jessica said. Atlanta, perhaps. It was warmer there, and the sporefall had been particularly dense.

Eridani 17 made no response, and its hand solidified. This meant that an alternate site was acceptable. Jessica would get a list of abandoned and near-abandoned cities to propose in tomorrow's negotiations.

Next on her agenda was a request for additional technology to assist in maintaining and rebuilding the human population in the regions hardest hit by sporefall. Negotiations happened in parallel, with dozens of humans in one-on-one sessions with the Eridani at any given time. She checked her tablet to make sure that nothing from the other sessions had altered her agenda.

"Like many of my people, I lost family members to the spore," Jessica began. She concentrated on her memories of her niece, a tiny baby that she had held only once. "We struggle to rebuild what we once had."

She was supposed to be asking for technological advances in transportation and communications, for new methods of agriculture to help human crops coexist with the invasive purple weeds that grew from the Eridani spores. She was supposed to infuse her spoken words with a plea for these things, so that the aliens would hear their needs in the spaces between her words. Instead, she thought of all the people she had lost in the sporefall and the chaos afterwards—relatives, coworkers, neighbors, friends.

Give them back, she pleaded. The Eridani were so advanced; there had to be something they could do. "Surely there is some technology you have that can help us."

Eridani 17 thinned itself entirely into cloud, leaving the purple sweater in a puddle on the floor. It reformed itself into the shape of

Gavin, her neighbor's four-year-old son who had died from the spore. The boy sat cross-legged on the floor and in his lap was a tightly swaddled baby with a drooly grin and dimpled cheeks. Lexi.

The alien had somehow called the children from her mind, but the scene that it created was not a remembered image. Gavin had never met Lexi. And yet, if he had, this was exactly how it might have looked. The boy's expression was a mix of curiosity and wariness, and Lexi—

She very nearly said what she was thinking, that she would give anything to have her back. Her death, and Ellie's breakdown, was destroying Oskar. Each death from the spore cascaded into a thousand unwanted consequences, and all the world was broken now. There must be some way the Eridani could undo time or reshape space and reverse the deaths they'd caused. There had to be a way.

Gavin held Lexi with one arm and raised the other up in front of him. He thinned his fingers, which was disconcerting. Jessica knew the ghosts were really just Eridani 17, but human fingers shouldn't thin the way that Gavin's were thinning.

"You will give us back the ones we've lost in exchange for," Jessica paused to study the map that hovered where Gavin's hand should have been. "The entire West Coast?"

It snapped Jessica back to reality. The Eridani had always shown remorse for what they'd done. They'd claimed to be unaware that the planet was inhabited, that they would not have sent their spore and, later, their colony ships, if they had known otherwise. She hadn't expected them to use her grief to their advantage in negotiations. She could not trade that much territory, not for mere ghosts.

"Not for shadows and memories," Jessica said.

Gavin leaned forward and kissed baby Lexi on the forehead. It was so close to what she wanted, they were almost real. Better than Ellie's empty bundle of blankets. Close enough, perhaps, to pull her sister-in-law back to reality. So close to what she wanted, and yet so far. And she couldn't trade that much territory even if the Eridani offered to pull the actual children from the past. "I am not authorized to negotiate concessions of this magnitude."

Gavin and Lexi melted right before her eyes, merged into a puddle, and reformed into the default frogform of Eridani 17. The entire session was recorded, and back on Earth it was undoubtedly already being analyzed. They would see the tears in her eyes, and she would be sent back to the planet in disgrace. Back to Earth, but not back home. Home was a place that still had those children in it.

Depression

Oskar got home from a long shift of weeding alien foodplants out of the avocado grove. His hands were stained purple and smelled of licorice. He set a 10 pound bag of avocadoes on the counter. He should trade some avocadoes to the neighbor kids for one of the trout they farmed in the courtyard fountain, but he didn't want to eat. He shut himself into his sister's guest bedroom and stared at the ceiling, crushed beneath the weight of his bad choices.

He shouldn't have left Ellie.

The walls were covered in sketches of his wife. Her smile, her eyes, her slender hands. Cheeks dotted with pale brown freckles. Hair tied back with a few loose strands to frame her face. She was the one who left him. She left reality behind and spent all day pretending a bundle of blankets was their baby girl. No one could blame him for not wanting to relive that kind of pain, day after day. He'd tried for months. Marybeth was a family friend, and he'd given her everything they had to take care of his wife.

All of that so Oskar could go and find his sister, Jessica. He'd been worried that she might need help, but she wasn't sitting helpless in her apartment. No, she'd gone off to the space station to be one of Earth's ambassadors. This was supposed to be his big chance to not be the baby brother anymore, to swoop in and save Jessica from the post-invasion chaos, and she hadn't needed him at all. She never did. He had no idea if she'd even gotten the message he'd tried to send.

Someone pounded on the door. Probably the neighbor kids. Brayden liked avocadoes, and trading with him was a better deal than trying to buy them somewhere.

He opened the door. "Jessica."

"I can't believe you changed my locks." Jessica faked a scowl, then grinned and gave him a big hug. "You look like crap."

Oskar retreated to Jessica's guestroom. His sister hadn't understood how he could come down here and leave Ellie behind, no matter how he tried to explain.

People started pouring in from the east. They moved into abandoned apartments, office buildings, malls. Los Angeles turned back into a bustling city. Jessica said that the government had traded Arizona and New Mexico to the frogs. All the extra people made it harder to get work. His heavy heart made it harder to wake up and face the day.

On his second straight day of refusing to get out of bed, Jessica marched into his room like she was twenty and he was ten, and she could boss him around. "Draw me a bird."

"Go away," he said. There were no birds, and he could see right through his sister's scheme. Birds were from happier times. She thought sketching a picture would pull him out of this funk. She was wrong. Remembering the way things were would only make it worse. "There are no birds. Sporefall killed them all."

"Think of it as rent. It'll do you good to draw something other than Ellie, over and over again. All I'm asking for is one really good picture of a bird." Jessica left without waiting for him to answer.

He only had a few sheets of good thick paper left, he'd used most of it to draw his pictures of Ellie. He got one out. He closed his eyes and tried to picture the stellar jays that had eaten peanuts from the feeder outside his window, back before the sporefall. He remembered blue and black feathers, and the general shape of the head, but the details were fuzzy. There were pictures of birds in books, but he shouldn't need that. He should be able to do this. It had only been a year.

For the first time in weeks, he opened the guestroom blinds. The apartment was on the fourth floor, and the window looked across the alley at a near-identical brick building. He tried to imagine birds flying in the alley, landing on the concrete below to hunt for bugs or seeds, but thoughts of flying set his mind to thinking about soaring out through the window and falling into oblivion.

He closed the blinds.

Two days later Oskar had only one sheet of good paper left, and he had not yet managed a picture of a bird. He ate when Jessica forced him to, and he slept until Jessica made him get out of bed. There was no point to pictures of birds. There was no point to anything, not anymore.

Jessica came in with half an avocado. Did he really have to eat, again? But no, she started eating it herself, spooning the mushy green into her mouth and smiling as though it actually tasted good to eat a plain avocado, again. "This is the last one from the bag, and food rations have been short at the community center, so we can't count on that. We need to decide what to do next. There's a caravan going north, right through Portland."

He didn't want to go back. What if Marybeth had abandoned Ellie, despite all her promises? He couldn't face the chance. "I'm staying here."

Jessica shook her head. "You're not. I'm trading the apartment for passage on the caravan and food for the trip. If you want to stay in L.A., you're on your own."

She left him to consider his options, and his gaze drifted to the window. It would be so easy, so quick. If he never went back to Ellie, he could believe that she was okay, maybe even happy. He wouldn't have to face a world that could never possibly be right again.

He opened the blinds. An alien was walking in the alley, smiling the same damn frog-smile that the aliens always smiled. It saw him in the window, and thinned into a cloud. When it came back together, it was a flock of birds. Not the stellar jays he'd been trying to draw, but pigeons, plump and gray. They fluttered up and landed on windowsills and power lines outside the window. They weren't real, but they were enough to evoke a clear memory in his mind.

Oskar could soar out the window, or he could draw this memory of birds for Jessica and go with her back to Portland.

He calmed his shaking hands and sketched the birds.

Acceptance

Marybeth walked with Ellie to the clinic. Ellie insisted on bringing 'Lexi,' a bundle of filthy blankets that she refused to believe wasn't actually her dead baby. Marybeth hoped the new treatment would help. Ellie was an amazing woman, able to find joy in all the smallest things. Even now, as they walked along abandoned streets with Eridani foodplants, Ellie chattered to her blanket-bundle baby about how beautiful the orange blossoms were on the lovely purple trees.

Marybeth couldn't appreciate the beauty of the 'blossoms.' They weren't flowers at all, but clusters of tiny spheres, each one full of orange spores. The trees would release spores soon, and despite Eridani assurances that there would be no harm to humans this time, she could not put aside her memories of the last sporefall, and all the death it caused. Yolanda's death.

Very few healthy adults had died in the sporefall, but her wife hadn't been healthy. She'd had alpha-1-antitrypsin deficiency emphysema—a genetic disease that left her with the lungs of a sixty-year-old smoker when she was only thirty-two. Even without the sporefall, her condition had been deteriorating. She'd had a complex daily routine of inhalers and pills to try to keep the coughing fits and wheezing in check, and a tank of supplemental oxygen for her worst days.

Yolanda would have seen the beauty in the alien plants, just as Ellie did. Looking at Ellie was like looking into Yolanda's past, back to the early days of their relationship, before her illness sapped away her strength.

Was falling in love with a straight woman any better than carrying around a bundle of filthy blankets?

The clinic was an Eridani clinic, one of several that were part of the treaty that had been negotiated with the aliens. They were greeted by a man in a white coat when they entered, and left to wait in a small room with black plastic chairs and battered magazines from before the sporefall.

"Will Oskar meet us here?" Ellie asked. Much as she refused to accept the death of her baby, she continued to believe that Oskar would return.

"He's not here, El. We're going to see one of the Eridani," Marybeth explained. "They have a treatment that might help you."

An alien appeared in the doorway, wearing what looked like a down comforter tied like a toga. It studied them with beady black eyes, then beckoned to Ellie, recognizing that she was the one more in need of treatment.

"I'd like to come too." Marybeth said.

The Eridani doctor nodded its assent.

The treatment was painful to watch. The alien thinned itself into a gray fog, then reformed into images drawn from Ellie's mind—not mindreading, exactly. If Ellie said nothing, the alien could not hear her thoughts. It was only when Ellie spoke about her daughter that the memories came through. Then it was like watching a moving slideshow all in shades of gray:

Oskar holding Lexi in the hospital, the day she was born.

Ellie's struggles with breastfeeding when Lexi wouldn't latch.

Bottles of formula, carefully mixed and warmed at all hours of the night.

So many things that Marybeth had never seen, memories that haunted poor Ellie and made her break from reality. Then came the worst, the sporefall.

Ellie going out to find formula for Lexi, and coming back covered in fine orange dust.

Lexi's pitiful coughing and weak cries.

The days on end where she only slept upright, leaning on Ellie's chest.

Finally, the end, the moment when there were no more breaths, and Oskar took Lexi away. Marybeth cried as the baby disappeared from the three dimensional scene the Eridani recreated from the particles of its own body. She glanced at her friend, hopeful that the therapy had helped. Ellie was crying, but she continued talking. Her baby was dead, but Ellie wasn't finished.

More images appeared, of a Lexi that never was, in a world that no longer existed. Lexi toddling across the living room, Lexi putting on a ridiculously big backpack and going off to kindergarten, Lexi at the park feeding ducks. There were no ducks, and Lexi would never be six, but the Eridani doctor showed the impossible futures right along with the horrifying past.

Lexi's senior prom, her wedding, the birth of Ellie's first grandchild. The scenes skimmed through time and Marybeth could no longer watch, no longer listen to Ellie's words. She simply watched Ellie stare into the images that poured out, and held Ellie's hand as she cried. Since she had turned away from the doctor, it took her a moment to realize that the Eridani had resumed its default frogform. Ellie was no longer speaking, only sobbing softly.

She met Marybeth's eyes, and there was a depth to her gaze that was missing before.

"My Lexi," Ellie said. "My Lexi is gone."

After the treatment, Ellie didn't need a caretaker, but Marybeth had long since abandoned her apartment and they enjoyed each other's company. Ellie often wore the same grim smile that so often graced Yolanda's face when she was sick, and it tugged at Marybeth's heart. She tried to remind herself that Ellie was a different woman, a *straight* woman, but she could not help but hope that somehow, if enough time passed, things could be different.

Ellie made good progress in embracing reality. Together they dismantled Lexi's crib and set it out on the curb in front of the apartment. It wasn't long before a woman who looked like she might be expecting came and carried it away.

Oskar came back from L.A. Marybeth greeted him at the door, and had no choice but to let him in, for all that he abandoned Ellie when she needed him most.

"I'm so glad you're both okay," he said. Marybeth shrugged. He could say what he wanted, it wouldn't change what he had done. She only hoped that she wouldn't lose Ellie, now that he was back.

"Hi, Oskar," Ellie said. The sight of him brought her to tears, but Marybeth couldn't tell whether they were tears of joy or pain or anger.

"I'm so sorry," Oskar said. "I didn't want to leave you, but I couldn't stay. I was hurting too."

"I forgive you," Ellie said. "I know it must have been hard."

He smiled and went to embrace her, but she stepped back. "I forgive you, but we can't go back to how things were. I saw what might have been, if the Eridani had never come, and Lexi had lived, and it was beautiful. We could have had an amazing life. But those are impossible futures, and I have to let them go and come back to what is real."

"Is it another man?" Oskar asked, then realized that Marybeth was standing there. "Or another woman?"

Ellie shook her head. "There's no one else. Certainly not Marybeth, though she's a dear friend."

It was nothing that Marybeth did not already know. She had always known that Ellie was straight; there had never been any sign that she was interested. Ellie would never be Yolanda.

Marybeth grabbed her coat and made polite excuses. Ellie and Oskar had a lot to talk about, and Marybeth didn't want to hear it. She went outside and started walking, not caring where she went.

The wind picked up, and an orange cloud blew down from the Eridani foodtrees. The second sporefall had begun, a new cycle of alien life. According to the translators, the initial sporefall had been a different strain, modified to be more aggressive for terraforming, so that the Eridani would be sure to have foodplants when they arrived at their new home. This second sporefall should be as harmless to humans as ordinary pollen.

Marybeth sneezed at the orange air, but she refused to go back inside. She would not hide from this new world.

ABOUT THE AUTHOR

Caroline M. Yoachim lives in Seattle and loves cold cloudy weather. She is the author of over two dozen short stories, appearing in such markets as *Lightspeed, Asimov's,* and *Daily Science Fiction,* among other places.

Bonfires in Anacostia

JOSEPH TOMARAS

1. The Table

On the left-hand side of the coffee table were stacked three Michael Chabon novels, one each by T.C. Boyle and Tim O'Brien, and a volume of Nathanael West's collected works. On the right were five guides to maximizing fertility, and two novels by Tessa Dare. In between were two stemless wine glasses.

The table itself was a clear polymer which, were it not encumbered with the remains of its owners' outmoded bibliomania, would reveal itself as a fully operational touchscreen. It was designed, however, to require replacement as soon as it received a hard thwack: The sort of urbane furnishing that only a childless couple would have purchased.

An advantage of this table, from the perspective of those charged with maintaining homeland security, is that its voice-activated features kept it in a continual state of attentive listening. If the owner kept it in its default, continuously connected networking mode—as 99% of purchasers of these models did—then every word spoken in its vicinity would fall under the expanded electronic surveillance authorization established by a certain executive order signed twenty years ago whose existence would be neither confirmed nor denied by anyone with legal authorization to know of it. That the owners happened to be Robert and Eileen Wexler, mid-level operatives in the DC office of the Cuomo 2024 re-election campaign, did not change the functioning of the table or of those analysts in Prince Georges County charged with making sense of its data-feed and hundreds of thousands more.

The table knew that objects totaling a weight of approximately ten kilograms were distributed unevenly across its surface, that the materials pressing against it were cloth, paper and glass, that Robert

15

had in recent weeks been putting the music of the Talking Heads, an American New Wave band active from 1975 through 1991, on heavy rotation, whereas Eileen preferred silence whenever she was in the room, and that at this instant they had just repaired to their bedroom to finish preparations for a dinner party at the home of Darius and Brandon Gartner-Williams. It also knew that they would sometimes clear enough space to pull up campaign memos, the Post and the Times (both New York and Washington, of each), polling results and Sunday morning talk shows on its screen. The table could not know what was contained within the archaic text delivery devices pressing against it, though it got occasional glimpses when Robert would leave a book open face-down atop it—a habit for which Eileen would chastise him each time, reminding him that it would damage the spine. Neither Robert nor Eileen knew that the table knew all these things, but neither did they trust it fully, which may account for their decision to reconnoiter the dusty shelves of the DC Public Library and that mildewy used book store in a garret two stories above the scrum of Adams-Morgan for some of their reading matter.

Robert entered the room, noted Eileen's glass adjacent to his, and snorted. "I'm pretty sure none of those books recommend sauvignon blanc to enhance your fertility."

"You try answering to Ari Levine all day without a bit of liquid assistance," replied Eileen as she joined him. "When's the party?"

"I couldn't even suffer Tyler Colson without my refreshment. Seven o'clock." The Wexlers' habit of carrying on two conversations simultaneously was either irritating or endearing, depending on whether one was in a relationship with similar idiosyncrasies.

"Besides," continued Eileen, sitting on the couch and lifting her glass. "It's no better for your sperm than it is for my eggs. What's on the menu?"

Robert paused a beat, as he decided it would be ill-advised to remind her of the test results showing that his forty-seven-year-old gonads were none the worse for wear. "I don't know. Brandon was freaking out when I called him this morning. He just found out that Camilo's new boy is a vegan."

"I need animal protein." Eileen took another sip. "Ari wanted me to work late. Try explaining to him that I needed to go to my husband's ex-boyfriend's party."

"Did you?"

"It's none of his business. I told him no amount of number crunching would change the situation: Short of a total catastrophe, Andy's got this locked up."

"Short of the rest of the country finding out that half the nation's capital is in flames, you mean."

"Exactly. It's out of our hands at this point."

Robert sat down. There was nothing left to say, but silence did not seem right, either. "We have an hour left before we have to go." More silence. "You could have a snack." Eileen was beginning to lean toward the table, and had not taken the hint. Robert stuck his hand beneath the belt of his slacks as if to adjust, but really, to direct her attention the way he wanted.

"We shouldn't dilute it," replied Eileen, not even turning toward him.

Robert bent down to the table, dragged his finger diagonally to define the dimensions of a window, and called up a live feed of the Senate floor.

It was not strictly accurate to describe Brandon as Robert's "ex-boyfriend," not with the connotations of past exclusivity that this conventional phrase carried. Brandon and Darius had been together since well before Robert had set foot in Washington; he came to live with them shortly after he started grad school at American, during their brief, turn-of-the-century experiment with polyamory. By the time Eileen, seven years his junior, started coming to the gatherings at the Dupont Circle brownstone—on the arm of Janet—the story had grown too complex and too far distant to be worth telling accurately. That they were still getting invited to what had become the most sought-after soiree among LGBT Beltway insiders, despite the apparent completeness of their switch to heterosexuality and the low visibility of their jobs—he was a fundraising database programmer, she a statistician—was testament to Brandon's forgiving nature, the increasing self-assuredness of the community, and Darius' reluctance to let go of anyone he knew would appreciate his jokes, stories and lectures.

Robert just needed to keep tabs on his alcohol consumption. The last time, someone had almost walked in on him and Camilo's last consort. He suspected Camilo had figured it out, and that this was why a new guest was coming to the dinner. There were three things to wonder about before going to these dinner parties: What would Brandon cook, what new anecdotes would Darius have, and how young and attractive would Camilo's current boyfriend be. As the senior senator from Ohio asked to be recognized by unanimous consent, Robert considered all three. Of this, the table had no inkling, and neither did Eileen.

"Can you believe the mouth on that kid?" After several hours of hibernation, the table was woken by the sound of Robert's voice.

"I know," said Eileen. "Actually what I can't believe is Darius."

"How so?"

"Well, all that stuff about the holograms and the riots and the fires." The utterance of three keywords in such rapid succession switched the table from passive data-gathering to active interface with the analytical mainframes at the Agency. Based on Robert's and Eileen's metadata signatures, the Darius in question was identified with a high degree of probability as the same Darius Gartner-Williams who was an analyst with the agency. "Some of that had to be classified."

"Darius has always known how to walk right up to the line without crossing it. That's the only way a raconteur like him could have stayed where he is for so long."

"I don't know, he just seemed, not upset, but maybe, yes, maybe upset, at what's going on in Southeast."

"You don't think he'd do a Snowden?"

"No way, not a chance. Forget I said anything." Robert found this injunction of Eileen's easy to follow, but not the table. The table is not programmed to forget.

From the rustling sounds of their clothes the table intuited that they had taken seats on the sofa. It could not tell, however, that Eileen was reaching for the fly on Robert's khakis. "Hey, I thought you said we shouldn't dilute," said Robert.

"Forget it. We're nowhere near the right part of the cycle."

"Is that the truth, or is that the wine talking?"

"Too much wine and not enough food. Can you believe it, lentils and vegetables?" A zipping sound, then a seeming non sequitur: "What did you think of Camilo's new boy?"

Robert flinched guiltily, as if somehow Eileen's question signaled some awareness on her part of his indiscretion with Camilo's last partner, but she wasn't looking at his face to notice it. "Too skinny. And how can someone that self-righteous be that racist?" Then after a pause, during which he realized that in fact he would love to watch that bigoted little twerp choking on his dick, but that he should not say anything to that effect to Eileen, as the intermingling of violence, hatred and sexuality would be unnerving to her, he took note of the increased exposure of his genitals to Eileen's manipulations: "Are you sure we should? Ooooh."

The table soon detected a gagging noise that seemed to emerge from Eileen's throat. "Before, aah, we go too far, ooh," continued Robert, "Nice finger work, uhh, ahh, could we try, anal?" The table knew he only ever asked this when Eileen was drunk.

"Sure."

"I'll get the lube."

"Don't bother going upstairs. Vegetable oil's fine."

After hearing some sounds emerging from the kitchen, the table detected the removal of ten kilograms of books and other assorted materials from its surface, followed by a pressure totaling about thirty kilograms coming from what appeared, from visual sensing, to be Eileen's torso. This impression was soon confirmed by ultrafast sequencing of DNA from one of her skin cells: This feature of the table's was not a major selling point, but when discussed was pitched as a security measure. What better way to track down a ten thousand dollar piece of home electronics, if stolen, than to have the thief's DNA sequenced and automatically sent to the police? What neither Robert nor Eileen realized was that the table was already in a heightened state of alert, as a result of the keywords Eileen had spoken just a few minutes before, and that the sequencer was not only on, but bypassing local law enforcement and communicating directly with the Agency.

After about fifteen minutes of further jostling, the sequencer also detected human coliform bacteria, and incomplete genetic material originating from Robert. We do not know what happened next, but it must have been especially vigorous: A critical component of the table's power supply was dislodged from its circuit, and we lost all signal.

2. The Duck

The first thing, always, was to take off the tie, open the foyer closet, and find an empty rod on the cedar tie hanger. The second was to take the kitchen apron out of the same closet, and put it on. The third was to proceed through the combined living room / dining room / hallway across the terra cotta tiling to the kitchen and dock his tablet in the countertop station. The fourth was to find the traffic report on the tablet. With these practiced movements, Brandon Gartner-Williams would clearly delimit his Inspector General self from his domestic Dupont Circle townhouse incarnation, and no matter how maddening the preceding workday had been, he would ready himself and his home and his dinner table for the arrival of his husband, Darius, or Dar for short.

The traffic report was the key, the moment at which uncertainty would take over from ritual and preparation, and the outside world would provide the information necessary to make the next set of choices and motions. For Darius worked as an analyst at a subdirectorate of the NSA whose name, existence, budget and mission were never acknowledged in public documents, at an office in the Maryland suburbs whose nondescriptness on maps and satellite images was so impeccable as to raise suspicion, and his way home required him to drive through the District's Southeast quadrant. The neighborhoods on the left bank of the Anacostia River had proven resistant to three decades of gentrification and were now the site of regular disturbances, but Darius had explained to Brandon that the traffic reports would be the only way to have any sense of what was happening. The agency had seen to it that the news would not spread to other metro areas, but the armies of functionaries, lawyers, military men, contractors and subcontractors who populated the more prosperous quadrants and suburbs of DC would not stand for censorship of their traffic reports. Cooperative discretion was all the agency demanded in this case.

Strictly speaking, Darius did not need to traverse Pennsylvania Avenue SE to get home. He could have taken the safer route, inching along the Beltway. But Darius was not one to swerve from an available straight line. At least, that was what Dar had told Brandon. Brandon suspected that Darius was insisting that he was no less black than the young men setting barricades and cars alight in the streets, that despite his Falls Church upbringing and UVA and Georgetown degrees that he had no less right to be in that neighborhood than those who were born and would likely die there.

Brandon suspected, but he never asked. Even though they had been together for nearly thirty years, had gotten married as soon as DOMA was overturned by the Supreme Court, had developed matching paunches and grown comfortable with each other's personhood, he still felt guilty for the casual hurts he had unwittingly inflicted in the early years of their relationship: The crestfallen gaze of a twenty-something size queen, disappointed to learn that a certain stereotype was not universally true, and other things, some more petty, others worse, that he cringed to recall. He had learned over time not to ask certain questions of Dar. He would listen when Dar had something to say, to get off his chest, but he would not ask.

It took a while for the traffic report to come on. The 501c4s had figured out a way to keep their ads from being blocked or noise-cancelled. In the 2024 election season, the machinery of constitutional government continued in full view of the populace, louder and brighter than ever. Brandon turned his thoughts to dinner.

He had the duck that he had been planning to make into a ragout over pappardelle for last night's dinner party, until he learned that Camilo's guest, a lithe sophomore from GWU, was a vegetarian. And not one of those "I'll just eat the salad" kinds, but some hysterical vegan who would take offense at the smells of flesh and fat, horrified at the holocaust of innocent animals to which he had been made a party. Camilo, a notorious chickenhawk, had pleaded with Brandon and Dar to change the menu. They made do with a cassoulet of autumn squash and Puy lentils, and a lot of Puligny-Montrachet.

He remembered the boy's comment that brought the party to a halt: "I don't understand why those people have to burn down their own neighborhood." Camilo dropped a fork. A dozen eyeballs made a circuit from the unexpected guest seated at the middle of the dining room table, to Dar at the head as always, to the ceiling. He went on, "I mean, not those people like, all African-Americans or anything like that, just those people in Anacostia."

Everyone knew Dar was going to lecture. When he was angry, he got professorial, an image that was helped by the leather-patched tweed jacket he had chosen for the evening. "Those people live in a neighborhood that is an embarrassment to this country, through decades of neglect. The government tried to bulldoze it into shape with urban renewal. Then the market took over, with gentrification, which is why you can live . . . where do you live again?"

"Columbia Heights."

"Why you can live in Columbia Heights and have no idea what it was like in the mid-nineties, when Brandon and I met. You remember, Bran?"

Put on the spot, Brandon had to speak, though he didn't want to. His response was clumsy, nervous and embarrassing. "When Dar and I met, we were both living on U Street. Even that was a little sketchy back then. No one would head up into Columbia Heights unless they had business being there, and the only people with business there were the junkies. Remember what I used to say about Anacostia, Dar?"

"Brandon was very new to DC. Back then the Green Line ended in Anacostia, and he would take it down to L'Enfant Plaza for work. He said the woman's voice on the Metro, before it was all computerized, made it sound like heaven."

Everyone laughed at Brandon's expense. Brandon excused himself: "She really did have an angelic voice."

Dar took no notice and continued. "I drive through that neighborhood every day, to and from work. Population density kept going up as people got priced out of everywhere else. The houses are falling apart, the roads are rutted like in any Third World country."

Camilo interrupted: "Like back home in Chile. Worse than Chile."

"It got better after Barack Obama was elected," Dar continued. "Some black professionals started moving in, fixing up homes, opening fancy restaurants. Bran and I even thought about buying a condo to shorten my commute to the new job, but, well, Brandon wouldn't exactly have fit in."

"Not that I would have minded living there, of course," protested Brandon, perhaps a bit too insistently.

"Of course, darling. Well, it's a good thing we didn't. The Second Depression started, half the gentrifiers lost their jobs and the other half moved back across the river as soon as some desperate fool pulled a knife on them. Then someone got the idea for holograms, a way to make it look to people flying into Reagan National or Dulles like there was not this lingering corner of squalor in the nation's capital. The people living there didn't seem to notice the illusions at first."

"I can't believe that they wouldn't notice," replied the boy.

"Believe or don't believe, it's up to you. But I see it every day in my job: Human beings will assume that things remain as they were, until they're forced to notice a change. The structures were ethereal, easy to miss if you don't think to look for them."

"So why the fires?" asked the boy.

"Some genius decided to throw a few white people into the mix, to try and jumpstart another wave of gentrification. You know the type. Young, artists or antiwar activists, skinny vegans . . . " Everyone tittered except the boy and Camilo, who did his best to mimic the disapproving earnest look on his young lover's face. "A few young bloods tried to earn their street cred by throwing punches at the strangers, and that's when people in the neighborhood realized something was happening. They started calling the images 'ghosts.' They noticed the shimmering patches in their roofs, the manhole covers in place of holes they had taught their children to avoid, the crackhouses and burnt-out lots that had become mansions. And someone—no one knows who, and I would know if anyone knew—tried to set one of the mansions on fire. And that was when they learned what it took government scientists a year and a million dollars to figure out: That fires disrupt the holoprojections. A well-aimed laser would do the same, anything that directs enough energy and light in the right place, but fires are more affordable. More democratic, if you will."

"I still don't see how that justifies the destruction. It just seems so stupid, counterproductive."

"They just want to be seen, their lives to be seen, as they really are. And I think *anyone* at this table"—Dar swept his hand broadly at the dinner party, consisting of four gay male couples, two pairs of lesbians, and a seemingly hetero couple who had, between the two of them, slept with half the other guests—"would understand wanting that."

But the lad was too born-in-the-twenty-first century to intuit the breadth of history that Darius had encapsulated with a single gesture, and soon enough, too soon, the word "animals" had been tossed out and Camilo made some excuses about the wine going to their heads and ushered his conquest out the door to his Adams-Morgan studio where there would doubtless be a glass-shattering fight, angry sex, or both.

So the upshot was, Brandon had to do something with that duck. If Darius had a short trip ahead of him, he would just break it down and sear the magrets for tonight so he could get something on the table quickly, then start tonight making confit with the legs for later, and freeze the rest of the carcass for stock over the weekend. If there were bonfires in Anacostia, he would have time enough to roast it. From what little Darius would let fall about his workdays, he understood that a quick dinner would have something to do with the operations branch of the subdirectorate—not Dar and the analysts, whom Dar represented as professional onlookers.

The ads had ended. Brandon listened to the traffic report with ears trained to listen for the unspoken.

3. The Car

Trayvon Allen, age twelve, was the lookout posted to watch the bonfire at the corner of Pennsylvania and 31st SE and alert the block to the arrival of police, fire department, the black cars, or anyone else who looked like they did not belong in the neighborhood. When he saw the black Audi making its way down an otherwise deserted stretch of Pennsylvania, he assumed it was operations, and flashed his mirror at the window of the 3rd floor apartment where DeShawn was camped out.

Something wasn't right, though. The car was coming at least sixty miles an hour, and accelerating. The driver seemed to be moving the steering wheel left and right, but the car stayed straight, as if someone had aimed it straight at the fire.

The driver didn't look right either. DeShawn came down with the crew and asked Trayvon, "Who that, T? Ops?"

"Naw, looks like some college nigga. Fat guy, glasses, faggoty suit."

The black Audi hit the bonfire, which had been built of cop cars, building lumber and gasoline, going at least eighty-five. They could hear the driver screaming from inside the car.

"Hold back, son," said DeShawn. "That shit gawn blow." DeShawn began walking backwards, hands above his eyes, and the crew mimicked. Then the gas tank on the Audi exploded, sending shrapnel into the holoprojector at the corner and shorting out the ghosts.

"Should we help him?" said Trayvon.

"He gone. Let's check him out before ops show."

The driver had smashed his own window and tried to climb out before the explosion. His dreads were still smoldering and the melted portions of his face looked bright pink against blue-black skin. He still had his ID and lanyard around his neck, the insignia of the agency visible from five feet away. "Shit, they gawn try and pin this on us," said DeShawn. "To the winds." At that signal, each member of the crew scattered in a different cardinal direction. Trayvon meandered south, swiping a half-burnt piece of paper off the ground. It had an address in the Northwest quadrant. He shoved it in his back jeans pocket.

By the time five black cars came west up Pennsylvania five minutes later, Trayvon, DeShawn and the other six members of the crew were all out of sight. Ten necks as thick as their heads, mostly white but two black dudes and a Latin among them: These were ops. Different crews, with older men or harder kids, would be sending down sniper fire any minute, but these guys were Kevlared head to toe.

Trayvon looked back at the scene from the Dumpster where he was hiding. Though the college-looking dude was one of their own, the ops looked neither surprised nor sad. He patted his rear pocket to make sure the paper was still there.

4. The Kid

Ordinarily a trip to Dupont Circle would be a simple matter of getting on the Metro, but things hadn't been ordinary in a long time. The Green Line had started bypassing all Southeast stations ever since the bonfires began, and the fare was well above Trayvon's hustle. If he had a flat map of the District in his mind he might have been able to calculate that the address was only a two-hour walk away. But the uprising and repression had warped his mental map of the city, transforming the Anacostia River into an impassable singularity. That he felt drawn to the address despite this wise caution was inexplicable through Trayvon's conscious thought. His path did not follow a straight line, but proceeded faster than a straight line trajectory would have taken him, as he slingshotted his way around obstacles known and observed: checkpoints, cop cars, black cars, vigilante gangs of yuppies in street mufti, and the cameras. For a black kid in an ash-stained white T-shirt, the District was more hazardous than an asteroid belt for the Millennium Falcon.

So by the time he arrived at the front door of the Gartner-Williams house, four hours had passed since the accident, agency representatives had come and gone, the duck, slightly overdone, had been sitting on the counter getting cold, Brandon's tears had pooled in a crease of the leather sofa on which he was lying, and Trayvon was starving. No lights were on in the house, and he hesitated before ringing the bell. Hesitated, but the same drive that had brought him this far led his finger to the button. The button activated not only the bell, but also a camera at the top of the doorway. If Trayvon had noticed the lens, he would have fled, but it was too dark on the street for him to suss it out.

Brandon hesitated before deciding to answer the door: It could, he reasoned, be the agency with more details on the circumstances of Darius's accident. Despite his decision, the ten-foot walk from the sofa onto which he had collapsed was like swimming through the Mariana Trench: slow and bone-crushing. In that time, Trayvon had multiple opportunities to re-consider, re-re-consider, and re-re-re-consider, and he had just begun to pivot his left foot away from the door when Brandon's voice creaked, raw, from the intercom. "Who are you? What do you want?"

The second question confused Trayvon a bit. For four hours he had undertaken this fool's errand contrary to his own conscious volition. "I ... I saw something," he said, retrieving the scrap of paper and holding it up to where, he now reasoned, the camera must be.

Brandon couldn't make out anything on the screen, but assumed it had something to do with Darius. His hope and trust opened the door before his fear could countermand it. "Come in. What did you see?"

"An accident. A black man in a black car. I found this." Trayvon stepped across the threshold and handed the paper to the white man with red eyes. Brandon recognized it as a scrap of a receipt from Darius' auto repair shop. "Did he live here?"

"Yes, he did. Please, come inside." Ordinarily, Brandon enjoyed being a host above all else. A twelve-year-old kid from the wrong side of town would not usually be on the guest list, but his instinctual hospitality overrode his mistrust and distracted him, momentarily, from his grief.

The smell of the duck reminded Trayvon of his hunger. He hadn't eaten anything since his sugar-cereal breakfast. "Smells good in here."

"Are you hungry?"

The thought crossed his mind that this white man could be a government agent, or a child molester, but his stomach growled in response. Admitting his poverty to this white stranger was out of the question, though, so all he said was, "I can eat."

"Come on in. I'll get you something to eat."

Trayvon followed Brandon into the kitchen. When they reached the counter, Brandon noticed that he hadn't turned off the tablet yet. He removed it from the dock and, with the same fluidity of motion with which he had started his kitchen prep earlier in the evening, hurled it against the exposed brick. The sudden violence and the crack of the screen made Trayvon jump back. "Why you do that?"

"I hate the news," said Brandon. He gestured at one of the stools opposite his work area. "Sit down. I'll cut you some duck. Do you want the leg or the breast?"

"I never had duck. Is it like chicken?"

"Yes and no."

"I'll try the leg."

"I didn't get a chance to cook any vegetables. I can make you a salad."

"Tha's'a'ight. I'll just try the duck." Trayvon wasn't sure if he'd ever eaten a salad, and he didn't want to have his first here. The white man and the duck were strange enough.

Brandon put a plate in front of him, then a fork and knife, and placed the duck leg on his plate. "What do you want to drink?"

"You got Kool-Aid?" Brandon shook his head, so Trayvon answered, "I'll just have some water."

"Sparkling or still?" Trayvon looked at him like he had grown a second head, so Brandon just ran an empty glass under the tap.

"The man in the car, what was he to you?"

Brandon set the glass in front of the kid and waited for him to look up into his eyes before answering. "He's my husband."

"You gay?" Trayvon, remembering his grandmother's lessons about being polite when folks offered their hospitality, had tried to suppress the hint of disgust in his voice, but he had failed.

"Yes, we're gay. Were gay. I am gay. Darius was my husband." This was Brandon's first attempt at applying past tense to Darius, and it ended in renewed tears. "Why did you come here?"

"I saw the accident, but it didn't look like no accident."

"What were you doing there?"

"I live there." Trayvon was not about to mention anything about his role in the construction and maintenance of the bonfires, comparatively minimal as it was, to this gay white dude. His husband had been with the agency, and for all Trayvon knew, so was this guy. Though he figured that if they worked at the same place they would have both been in the same car, but that didn't mean this guy wasn't still government. Government was all over the place.

"What did you mean, it didn't look like an accident?"

"Like, he was trying to turn the car, trying to steer the wheel, I saw him, and I'm sure he was trying to slow down, too. But the car kept going straight, and faster. Like someone had set it up that way."

"He wouldn't have died if your friends hadn't set up the bonfires."

"I don't know nothing about no bonfire," lied Trayvon. "And nobody I know, knows how to make a car do that," he said, returning to the truth. "I just came here 'cause I figured, if he had peoples, they might want to know what I seen."

Brandon sat silently, shaking his head every minute or so as a new thought occurred to him. After the first headshake, Trayvon started eating the duck. After the second, Brandon pulled a piece of crispy skin off the carcass, folded it, put it in his mouth, and started chewing, his only bite since the agency had informed him of the "accident."

After several minutes of silence, Trayvon had finished the duck leg. "Thanks," he said. "That was some good shit. I'm'a go home."

"It's well after curfew, kid. The cops'll arrest you. You can stay here."

"Where?"

"You can have the bed. I'll stay out here, sleep on a couch, if I can sleep at all. I've been thinking so much about Darius, I realize, I've completely forgotten my manners. We haven't been properly introduced. What's your name?"

Trayvon hesitated, considering whether he wanted to sleep in a bed where *two dudes done all kinds of nasty gay shit*, or whether he wanted this one to know his name, weighing the unknown risks of each against the known risks of being a twelve-year-old black kid out after curfew. "Trayvon," he said.

"Are you named after . . . ?"

"Yeah. I was born the year he died. Momma liked the name."

"Hi, Trayvon. I'm Brandon," said Brandon, extending his hand. Trayvon shook. "It's not safe for you to go back out before the morning. Please, rest here."

Trayvon's legs and feet reminded him of the fatigue of his six-mile walk. "A'ight." Brandon pointed the way to the bedroom. Once Trayvon found the bed, he fell face first into it and went directly to sleep, in t-shirt and jeans, smearing soot onto the duvet.

5. The Wake

It was ten o'clock in the morning, and Camilo's lover Travis was still asleep, completely naked, and lying on top of the comforter. Camilo had been awake for two hours, and in that time had showered, made coffee, cooked breakfast, eaten breakfast, gotten dressed, and dug around in his stash for a bottle of pisco he could bring to Brandon and Darius' house—scratch that, now it was just Brandon's, he had to remember—as a means of comfort. He had spent the last five minutes watching the sweat pool in the curve of Travis's lower back and his shoulders rise and fall with each breath. Now his patience was at an end. He considered rimming the young man, as a kind way to wake him, but quickly ruled it out. For no reason he could discern, he felt as though Travis's contretemps with Darius must have had something to do with yesterday's accident. He was angry, and it wasn't the kind of anger that he could express through fucking. Holding the pisco bottle by its neck, he prodded Travis in the shoulder with the bottom.

"Wake up, already! Wake up! Levantate!"

"What the hell, C? It's Saturday."

"I told Brandon we'd be there in the morning. The morning's almost finished."

"I didn't like him."

"Who? Brandon?"

"Naw, Brandon's alright."

"Darius isn't even cold in the ground, and you're talking shit about him? He was my friend. We're going to help Brandon out."

Travis pulled on last night's clothes, and they made the twenty minute walk down to Brandon's in silence.

The doorbell woke Trayvon. Brandon, having hardly slept, was in the kitchen brewing more coffee. When he opened the door, Camilo spoke first. "How you holding up, Bran?"

"Not so good, Camilo. It's good to have friends around."

"I'm sorry for your loss," offered Travis.

"Thank you . . . . What was your name again?"

"Travis."

"Thank you, Travis. My mind's just been . . . "

"Of course, Brandon," said Camilo. "Let's go inside. Is anyone else here yet?"

"No, nobody at all. Bobby and Eileen are coming soon, and Susan, too, but Cassie has to work today." As they traversed the foyer, Trayvon entered the open kitchen.

"Is that nobody?" asked Travis.

"Oh, my god, I forgot," muttered Brandon. Then he called, "Trayvon, let me introduce you to my friends." Trayvon approached hesitantly. "This is Camilo, and this is . . . "

"Travis," said Travis, who remained aloof. Camilo offered his hand not in a shake, but as if to try and draw the boy's hand up for a kiss, an offer not taken by Trayvon.

"Trayvon saw the accident."

"Ay!" gasped Camilo.

"So he's one of the rioters, then?" said Travis.

"I think I should be going," said Trayvon, assuming the most proper, schoolroom tone of voice he could recall. "Thank you for letting me stay here, mister."

"Brandon," insisted Brandon.

"Thank you, Mister Brandon."

"No, please, stay. My friends are coming over for brunch, and I want you to tell them what you told me last night, about Darius."

"I don't know if I should."

"There's nothing to worry about, Trayvon. My friends know powerful people who should know the truth. We can keep you safe."

"Have you ever had a pisco sour, son?" asked Camilo, brandishing the bottle.

"He's way too young, Camilo. Twelve."

Camilo looked down at his shoes, reassuring himself that the boy looked mature for his age, then offered: "I'll make you one, Bran."

"Too early, Camilo. But let's go in, and you can be a dear and put a splash into my coffee."

6. The Bridge

The surveillance cameras on the Frederick Douglass Memorial Bridge across the Anacostia River were knocked out by a power outage just after six p.m. on Saturday. The cause of the outage did not need to be investigated, since everyone whose responsibility it would be to investigate it was already disposed to attribute it to a nearby bonfire.

When the body of Trayvon Allen was discovered the following day in Fort Hunt, on the Virginia side of the Potomac River, anyone who was in a position to investigate his cause of death saw plainly that it was due to a fall from a great height. If he was taking a circuitous route from the Dupont Circle area to his home in Congress Heights, he might very well have been crossing the Douglass bridge during the time when its surveillance cameras were out.

No bullets were recovered from his body. We repeat: No bullets were recovered from his body. Anyone who says otherwise is engaging in irresponsible speculation.

ABOUT THE AUTHOR

Joseph Tomaras now lives in a small town in southern Maine, following sojourns of varying length in New York City, Washington DC, Durham, Nashville, Urbana-Champaign, Binghamton, Albany, Great Barrington, Lake Placid, the indistinguishable suburban expanses of Palm Beach County (Florida), Athens (Greece) and Los Angeles. His fiction has appeared in *The Big Click* and *FLAPPERHOUSE,* with other pieces soon to appear in *Phantasm Japan* (Haikasoru) and *M* (Big Pulp). His opinions on the precise shape and trajectory of our present handbasket can be found at skinseller.blogspot.com, and he masochistically encourages strangers to yell at him on Twitter (@epateur).

The Saint of the Sidewalks
KAT HOWARD

Joan wrote her prayer with a half-used tube of Chanel Vamp that she had found discarded at the 34th St. subway stop. It glided across the cardboard—the flip side of a Stoli box, torn and bent—and left her words in a glossy slick the color of dried blood: "I need a miracle."

You were supposed to be specific when asking the Saint of the Sidewalks for an intervention, but everything in her life was such a fucking disaster, Joan didn't know where to start. So, she asked for a miracle, non-specific variety.

She set her cardboard on the sidewalk, prayer-side up. Then lit the required cigarette—stolen out of the pack of some guy who had been hitting on her at a bar—with the almost empty lighter she had fished out of the trash. You couldn't use anything new, anything you had previously owned, in your prayer. That was the way the devotion worked: found objects. Discards. Detritus made holy by the power of the saint.

Joan took a drag off the cigarette, then coughed. She hadn't smoked since her senior year of high school, and she'd mostly forgotten how. Thankfully, she didn't have to actually smoke the thing. Cigarette burning, she walked three times around her prayer, then dropped the butt to the sidewalk, and ground it out beneath her shoe.

Then she waited to see if her prayer would be answered.

Other people waited too, scattered along the sidewalk where the saint's first miracle occurred, with their altars of refuse and found objects, prayers graffitied on walls, or spelled out with the noodles from last night's lo mein.

The rising sunlight arrowed between the buildings, and began to make its progress down sidewalks lined with prayers. This was how it worked: if the sun covered your prayer, illuminating it, the saint had heard you. There was no guarantee of an answer, but at least you would know you had been heard. For some people, that was enough.

If your prayer caught fire, if holy smoke curled up from its surface as the sun shone down on it, that was a sure sign you had been blessed. Heard and answered, and your intention would be granted. A miracle. If she just had a miracle, things would be better.

Joan didn't need to watch to follow the progression of the sun. Cries of disappointment and frustration were common. Gasps of joy and gratitude much rarer.

Everyone had theories about how the saint chose to grant prayers. Some said it was whether she liked the altar, or the things you used to make your prayer. Others said she could feel the need in your heart, and mend your broken life that way. Joan hoped it was the latter, since it wasn't like her hasty scrawl and filthy cardboard was that impressive. Certainly not compared to what was next to her—a salvaged player piano, painted with neon daisies, tinkling through a double time version of "Music Box Dancer." Though really, Joan hoped the saint had better taste than to pick that one.

She tapped the toes of her left foot on the sidewalk as she waited, just below the cigarette. Maybe it was bad form to be impatient about a prayer, but Joan didn't care. She just wanted to know. Plus, she really had to pee.

The sun crept closer, the light crawling over her ancient Docs. It licked up her legs, over her chest, illuminated her hair, a brief halo.

Then paused, on the sidewalk again, inches from her prayer. Joan bit her lip hard. Come on, come on, come on, she chanted inside her head. Please.

A drop of rain. Then another and another. The sky greyed, then grew storm-dark. The opened, rain sheeting down. The worst of all possible signs.

Soaked to the skin, Joan ran into a coffee shop. She shouted her order as she passed the counter so she could use the "For Paying Customers Only" toilet. After she washed her hands, she rubbed the smeared mascara—waterproof her ass—from beneath her eyes.

Well then. No miracle. She would figure out something else.

The voices woke Joan the next morning. A crowd of people outside of her apartment, congregating on the sidewalk, on the steps. She angled her head to better see out of her sliver of window.

There were the beginnings of altars, but these were made to honor some sort of saint she had never seen before—coffee cups and lipstick cases, worn Docs and tights with holes. The hair on the back of her neck stood up.

Joan checked her Book of Hours, but there were no saints scheduled to appear on her street today. It wasn't a feast day, either.

She shrugged into a thrift store kimono, worn at the hem and wrists, but its embroidered peonies still bright, and went down to see what the fuss was about, hoping she was wrong.

"Our Lady of the Ashes!" "Our Lady of the Lightning Strike!" greeted her as she opened the door.

The people outside had smeared ashes on their faces, were waving scorched pieces of cardboard like holy relics. Most had painted their lips with dark lipstick. The front line of them fell to their knees before her.

"Oh, fuck no," Joan said, and fled back into her apartment.

Joan hadn't been online to do more than check her email in over a week. Nine days ago, she discovered that her (now ex) boyfriend was cheating with her (now former) best friend, which would have been bad enough on its own, but Joan had still been drunk and angry enough the day after to punch the asshole who liked to grab her ass when they were in the elevator together. Except. Said elevator was at work, and said asshole was her (now former) boss. Joan had gotten fired.

On reflection, it had not been her finest twenty-four hours.

In the wake of all of that, she hadn't wanted to scroll through social media feeds full of pity and snark, or pictures of the happy new couple—because, of course, the best friend and the boyfriend were in love—so she hadn't looked at anything.

She did now.

She had run fast enough ahead of the storm that she hadn't seen it happen, but lightning had struck the cardboard on which she had written her prayer. Had scorched it, but had not consumed it. Even stranger—although the cardboard had been prayer-side up, her words had been seared onto the sidewalk, still in the same shade of elegant goth Chanel lipstick she had scrawled them in.

Nothing else had been touched.

People were already calling it a miracle. Apparently every major department store in the city had sold out of Vamp, it was backordered online, and tubes were going for upwards of $100 on eBay.

Joan closed her laptop. "This is too weird," she said. She looked out of her window again. There were even more people out front. She shrugged into a hoodie, and pulled the hood tightly over her hair. Then she slunk out of the back of the building, holding her breath against the stench, and very carefully not looking at the spatters and smears as she passed the dumpster.

Things were even crazier on the street where she had made her offering yesterday. Her *rejected* offering. Because whatever this was that was happening, it was not how the Saint of the Sidewalks worked. No one had ever heard of her making a new saint before.

Ash-smeared people wearing blood-red lipstick waved scorched pieces of cardboard. Some were calling out "Saint Joan of the Lightning! Strike us!"

Great. Not only did they know where she lived, but they knew her name. Joan pulled her hood tighter over her head, and walked as fast as she could back to her building.

That was how saints were made. Some piece of strangeness happened, and it hooked itself in the heart of someone who saw it, and called it a miracle. Once they decided that's what it was, people tried to reenact the miracle's circumstances. They ritualized its pieces. They named the person at the center of it, gave them an epithet, something memorable.

The Saint of the Sidewalks had been a homeless woman, with a pile full of belongings, broken and worn. Perhaps relics from her previous life, perhaps more recent scavengings. She sat on it like it was her throne.

One day, it caught fire. Spontaneous combustion, said the witnesses. Too hot and fast to save her.

Except. No body was found. Surely a miracle, in and of itself. But then the stories started, saying that everything the fire touched had been made whole, restored. And so she became the Saint of the Sidewalks, her altars made of broken things, refuge her relics, and prayers sent to her in fire and smoke.

Joan did not want to be a saint.

The crowd at the front of her building had grown even larger, and there were peonies, baby pink and fuchsia and striated with color, woven through the handrails on the front steps. Those gave her pause for a moment, then she realized—the pattern on her kimono. Scary, that that was all it took.

The press of people was terrifying, the number of them, the fervency. She could feel the want, the terror and desperation, rising from them in waves. It made her dizzy, seasick, and again, Joan slunk in through the back entrance, trying to remain unnoticed.

Joan thought she heard someone yell her name, but she pulled hard against the door, not letting go until she felt the lock engage, and then ran up the steps to her apartment.

She had forty-one new emails, thirty-six direct messages on Twitter, and there were four hundred seven new pictures that she was tagged in on Instagram. She herself was only in thirteen of them. The rest were her building, the lightning-struck sidewalk where her prayer was.

Almost all of the messages and tags were requests for prayers, for interventions, for help.

Joan didn't even make it through ten of them before she wanted to punch something—the world, maybe—and a few more after that and she was crying. Hot, angry tears, that these people were so desperate as to see her as their best option.

She wasn't. She didn't even know how to fix her own life, much less theirs. The lightning had struck her prayer, not her—she had no superpowers. She was just a woman with a cheating ex, no job, and no coffee in her apartment.

Joan ordered in groceries and promised an obscene tip if the delivery person would meet her at the back. Nine text messages from her ex came in while she waited, all variations on how he was "So sry, bb." Not sorry enough to type entire words, apparently.

Plus, he was selling the cardigan she had left at his place on Craigslist, calling it a holy relic. He was also not sorry enough to just give it back to her when she asked him for it, the dick.

Getting the groceries was a fiasco. The crowd of people had found the back of her building, and by the time she had gotten back inside, three of her eggs were smashed, someone had stolen her grapes, and she had gotten smeared with ashes, her arms covered in people's handprints. She wondered if yelling "Get the fuck away from me, you fucking freaks!" would make people see her as any less of a saint.

She wondered if they'd see her as normal if they saw her hiding in her bathroom, wiping away tears, or if they'd just hold out vials to collect them in.

For some people, the saints were like candles bought at bodegas: a series of interchangeable names etched on glass, to be forgotten when the too-vivid wax burnt down. They were the equivalent of love spells found on the internet, tarot cards bought to be party tricks.

If Joan was honest, that's what they had always been for her. Even the intention that had gotten her into this mess—"I need a miracle"—had been desperation, not piety. In the darkest part of her heart, she hadn't really expected anything to happen, even if the sun had immolated her request. She had hoped something would happen, sure, but the gesture had been more of a way to feel like at least she had done something, than out of any fervent belief.

It was after midnight now, and raining, and there were still people clustered around the doors to her building. She had been braced all day for management to complain, but the message that pinged her inbox hadn't been a noise warning, but an offer of a month's free rent. The publicity her presence generated had been a real boon. Oh, and he'd be happy to get her oven fixed, too. (It spontaneously turned off after twenty minutes, no matter what temperature it was set to. Joan had put in the maintenance request three months ago.) He just had a quick prayer he wanted to send her way. Joan looked away from it. It seemed too intimate, to read what someone was praying for.

There was a GIF of a lightning strike at the bottom of the email.

Joan typed "Yes"—meaning the rent and the working oven—and copy-pasted the GIF, because she didn't know what else to do with it. She felt sick to her stomach. She wasn't a saint, she wasn't, but this had to be better than just ignoring the guy, right? She hit send.

Blue-white lightning cracked outside her window.

There was a crash. A scream. Then cheering.

"Saint Joan of the Lightning!" they cried.

She did not get up. She did not look.

Joan sat at her computer, staring at the "message sent" icon, hands covering her mouth. I need a miracle, she thought.

This time, the voices that woke Joan weren't from the chaos outside. They were in her head. People begging, beseeching: "Strike me with your holy fire, lady." "I cover myself in ashes until I am worthy of your light." Other things she understood less—languages she didn't speak, incoherent weeping. She sat up in bed, and clung to her blankets.

This was insane. She was no saint. She couldn't answer prayers. Didn't want the responsibility. Certainly didn't want other people's fucking voices inside her head.

She opened up her laptop, and started to type.

Turns out, once people decide you're a saint, they're reluctant to let you stop being one. They retrofit your actions to their desired narrative. So even though Joan wrote an explanation to her followers—ugh, that word—that she was just like they were, denied all ability to help people, to work miracles, they took her words as a sign of humility, of caring, of becoming modesty. The devotion to her only increased. She couldn't walk anywhere without prayers reverberating in her head.

The constant press of people sent her into trembling panic attacks, and so she lied, said that any unwanted physical contact would shock people, a result of the lightning that still passed through her.

She'd picked the ability because she wished she'd had it around her grabby ex-boss. But the story spread, and people gave her space. Almost enough that she could breathe.

Joan was never sure, after, how it happened. If the man had acted deliberately or not. But there was a hand on her upper arm, and then there was a spark and snap, and then there was a man, flung backwards, heaped up against a wall.

Joan stood, frozen to the spot. The man scrambled to his feet, then prostrated himself before her on the sidewalk. Already, the branching tattoo of the lightning strike was visible on his skin. He apologized and begged her forgiveness.

She gave it to him, of course. That was what saints did.

"It gets worse, the more they believe in you, not better." The woman sat on a stoop, bright fuchsia sequined Converse scattering sunlight from beneath the hem of an unbelted cream trench coat. "All of the supernatural bullshit, I mean."

"How do you know that I"—Joan started.

"You look haunted. Hollow. Like people have been biting off pieces of your insides.

"Plus, you're all over the internet. Our Lady of the Lightning."

There was a clink, as the piece of a shattered flowerpot replaced itself, making the terracotta whole again. A sensation like flame passed over Joan's skin.

Down the block, a flat bicycle tire refilled itself, and the bent wheel of a homeless man's shopping cart straightened.

Refuse made whole. Tiny, spontaneous miracles of proximity, accompanied by the heat of flames that did not consume what they touched. Joan felt pretty sure she knew who she was sitting next to.

"Right. Of course. What do you mean, it gets worse?" Joan plucked at a torn cuticle, worrying the skin until it bled, then winced at the pain.

"The more they believe, the more you become a part of those beliefs. Or did you think hearing voices and being electric were just talents you picked up?"

Joan shook her heard. "Does it stop?"

"Maybe. If you're lucky." There was longing in the woman's voice.

"I only wanted a miracle," Joan said.

The woman stood up, her shoes blinding in the sun. "And what makes you think you didn't get it?"

For the first time in her life, Joan desperately wanted to pray. To pray fervently, devotedly. To light candles before an altar, to obscure the sand of a mandala with her feet.

And she couldn't. Every time she opened her Book of Hours, every time a text alert popped up on her phone to notify her of a holy day, she thought of someone else, trapped by the weight of people's desires. Someone who, like her, could not sleep without being woken by voices raised in prayer, who could not leave their apartment without becoming the unwilling head of an impromptu pilgrimage.

She couldn't pray, not when doing so might trap someone else.

So she left. Joan wasn't sure if you could abdicate sainthood, but she would try. She hoped that if she could just get far enough away from the ecstasy of belief, find somewhere that people didn't know her face or care where she lived, she could go back to being normal.

She dyed her hair in her sink. She left in darkness. She used the last of her tube of Vamp lipstick to scrawl "Do not Look for me. I will not be Seen." on her mirror and she left the door to her apartment wide open.

She did pack her peony covered robe. She really liked it.

And then she ran.

Far, far away from where things began, Joan watched as the devotees of Saint Joan of the Lightning staged a service in her honor.

They wore masks now, that completely obscured their eyes, so that they could not accidentally see her. It had been that, more than the distance, that had helped—she could grocery shop in peace, most days, and usually the people who recognized her only thought she looked familiar. They didn't quite know why. And if she had peony plants in her yard, well, so did most people. She stood out less, having them.

She watched on her laptop screen as they slicked dark lipstick over their mouths, then wrote their prayers on pieces of cardboard and pressed them to the sidewalk. She thought she saw a pair of fuchsia sequined Converse walk through the crowd, and she smiled.

Joan felt the hair raise on her arms, felt static electricity crackle across her skin. She would hear the voices—she had learned to listen without going mad, to separate out the pleas—and when she heard people asking for their own miracles, she touched her screen and struck their prayers with lightning, burning them to ash, letting hope rise up like holy smoke.

She was very careful to only choose the most specific prayers. She knew very well that without direction, miracles were never what you expected them to be. She watched her own, and touched her finger to the computer screen. In a crackle of lightning, at a distance, a prayer was answered.

ABOUT THE AUTHOR

Kat Howard is the World Fantasy Award-nominated author of over twenty pieces of short fiction. Her work has been performed on NPR as part of Selected Shorts, and has appeared in *Lightspeed, Subterranean,* and *Apex,* among other venues. Her novella, *The End of the Sentence,* written with Maria Dahvana Headley, will be out in September from Subterranean Press. You can find her on twitter as@KatWithSword

The Rose Witch
JAMES PATRICK KELLY

Most in that country called Tzigana a witch, though never to her face. Now that she was dead, you would expect that the girls who had lived in her tumbledown house might say whatever they wished. But none dared speak against the old woman. All but one continued to bless her memory, constructing imagined kindnesses out of blankets as thin as soldiers' socks, candle stubs dipped from scrap wax, and joints of stringy goat for the turnip soup. They even pretended to mourn. Julianja was disgusted by their cold tears, but she kept quiet and watched for what would happen next. She respected and feared Tzigana, even now. If the old woman rose from the dead to snatch a girl for company in the tomb, Julianja wouldn't have been surprised.

What was to become of them? Dorottya, the elder of the twins, had taken charge, but she had neither the experience nor the sense to run a household. They were seven girls, ranging in age from eleven to twenty, all little better than servants. Tzigana had taken them on as apprentices, yet she had shared little of her arcane knowledge. Frici could spark fire from the tips of her forefingers and Zsuzsanna could draw the ache from strained muscles and Julianja could make roses breathe, but these skills wouldn't pay for the meat or salt or shoes they needed.

Dorottya declared they must seek work away from the house and sent the girls to trade with the houses of men. They offered to sew and bake, tend vegetable patches and put up preserves, chop wood and sweep floors. Julianja knew this plan would never succeed. The women who lived with men would not welcome needy girls. For her part, Julianja refused to leave the old witch's garden, since it was the only light in her dim life. No argument or censure would move her.

You may be right to despise Tzigana. In life, she neglected most of what we hold dear. She let magic consume her and paid as little heed to

40

the house as she did to history or the troubles of her country. Certainly she loved her roses more than the girls who were her charges. But she had used her wits to impose her austere order on the world. While hers was rarely a joyous place, no one there went hungry. No one took sick, thanks to the witch's charms. The girls might complain, but they stayed until they were sent away. Each was treated equally so they might become their truest selves, away from the plans and strictures and desires of men. And of course Tzigana's garden drew noble visitors. She left the world more beautiful than she found it. How many of us can say the same?

The girls seemed to be managing without their mistress, although Julianja wasn't fooled. The house was but two days' walk from the town of Szeged and a few of the girls found work nearby, especially pretty Erzebet. But then boys started following them back to the house. Dorottya knew enough not to let the rascals in, but they would climb the chicken coop and call through the windows. They soon learned better than to try to cut through Julianja's roses; she was merciless with her birch switch.

By the time the roses bloomed, the garden was hers alone. The other girls were either too busy or too lazy to help Julianja tend it. Where once she had hung back while the witch had greeted the seekers who came to her garden, now she waited by herself at the gate to receive them. With Tzigana gone, however, only a few came.

The frail bishop arrived swaddled in furs and bundled in a horsehair blanket and still he looked cold and blue, even in the heat of early summer. He staggered to a Damask rose, which presented in delicate sprays of semi-double flowers. Tzigana claimed that it came from stock which the Crusader King András himself had brought back from the Holy Land; it was red as blood of infidels. The bishop wheezed as he breathed in its scent, then pressed his usual *denar* into Julianja's hand and left without another word. The boar prince spoke only German but indicated his preference for the pink cabbage rose by snuffling at it with his blunt snout. Afterwards he scrabbled back into his golden palanquin and was borne away by his four squires without leaving so much as a copper.

In the past, there had been almost as many women as men visiting, but that year only the dowager Baroness came in her dusty carriage. She peered at Julianja over her glasses, the left lens of which was cracked down the middle.

"Is she sick?"

Julianja met her watery gaze boldly. "Dead."

"No." The woman gasped and cupped hands to the sides of her head, as if she could not hear through her wimple. "Dead?"

"It was Palm Sunday. We were at Mass."

"Did she say anything?"

"She told Dorottya that her legs were cold. As she rose to receive the Sacrament, she collapsed."

"I mean about me."

Julianja shook her head.

"She should have forseen this. Now who will take care of the roses?"

"I will." Julianja ground her bark sandal against the path, staking out her claim. "As you see."

The dowager gave an unhappy laugh. "You can try." She gestured with her walking stick. "Take me there." Her special mountain rose was a particular favorite of the bees. It was a climber, the flush of creamy blossoms carried high. Julianja went up on tiptoes and brushed the bees away with the back of her hand, then bent one of the stems toward her. The thorns of this rose were mere prickles and she had to worry at one until she had stabbed her forefinger deep enough to draw blood. She watched the bead grow before pointing at the closest bloom and blowing a spray of blood at the crown of yellow stamens.

"Be quick about it," commanded the dowager.

Still holding the stem, Julianja twisted away to make room. She braced for a lash across the legs that did not come. Instead, the dowager brushed past her and buried her face in the charmed flower Her snuffling reminded Julianja of the boar. When her head lolled away, Julianja released the stem and it sprang into place.

Tzigana had first used Julianja to create the rose charm three summers ago, after she had sent Vica away. Year after year the girl had watched as the highborn had been transported by the mingling of her blood and the perfume of the blossoms, and yet never understood how it happened or what they felt. She'd always wanted to know, but Tzigana had laughed whenever she asked. Or cursed her. But Tzigana was in her tomb.

"What is it?" said Julianja. "Tell me."

The dowager shivered as if awakening from a dream and then thrust her face close to Julianja's. The crack in her glasses made her left eye seem to be doubled. "How old are you?"

Julianja's mother had sold her to Tzigana when she was but a child, and if the witch knew the day of her birth, she had never said. Julianja had started bleeding last summer, and Zsuzsanna said that meant she was sixteen, but Frici said no, she might be fourteen or even seventeen. Every girl had a different time. "Old enough," she said.

"Maybe you are." The dowager pinched Julianja's breast. "Have you been with a boy yet?"

She slapped at the woman's hand twice before she let go. Julianja would have slapped her face, but the woman thrust the knob of her walking stick at the girl to ward the blow off.

"No matter. If the old woman is truly gone, then her garden must die." She fumbled with the drawstrings of her purse and dropped a handful of *denars* into a patch of speedwell. "These roses don't want you, peasant."

Julianja had been trying not to see this. While the rest of the garden bloomed as usual, the roses were failing. She'd been fighting brown canker since the canes had first come into bud, and she'd spent the last week stripping away leaves infected with the powdery mildew. The sulfur dust that Tzigana had left was nearly gone and there was no money to buy more. Only the humble dog rose, scrambling up the cherry tree, had been spared. Dorottya talked about pulling up the sick plants and giving the space over to paprika peppers. The girls could dry the chilies, grind them and sell the spice that fall at market. The idea made Julianja furious.

As June gave way to July, she worked harder to save the roses. One hot day she was at the fence, pruning dead wood from a pink rambler that had once covered the rails in every direction. She wore only her shift against the heat; damp coils of hair matted against her forehead.

"Hello *bogárkám*." Nandor, the carpenter's son, had big feet and a silly grin, which always got sillier whenever he saw Julianja.

"I am not your little bug. Go away. None of the girls are home today."

"Except you." He leaned across the fence.

"That's saxifrage you're crushing, blockhead."

He clasped both hands to his chest. "And it's my heart you're crushing, dear girl." His face was pale and as big as the moon.

When she reached for her birch switch, Nandor danced backwards, laughing. "I will submit to your lash gladly," he said, hands held high in the air, "if only you'll submit to mine."

They both heard the creaking before they saw the cart. And they spotted the mule before they glimpsed the knotted man.

"Be on your guard, Juli," said Nandor in a low voice. "These beggars are everywhere. First they ask for what is not theirs, then they steal it."

The knotted man wore a homespun tunic over an undershirt; his dun breeches came to the knee and his lower legs were wrapped in linen. But what you would have noticed first about this traveler were the knots, some for show, some necessary. His tunic was held closed by strips of tied leather and was fringed with knotted wool. He wore a finely braided rope for a belt, and a silk scarf secured around his neck against the dust of the road. He had a boy's face with only a scraggle of beard but his long black hair was tied in a topknot in the soldier's style. They say that this makes the warlike seem fiercer, or at least taller. But the knotted man carried no weapons. For her part, Julianja was struck by the set of his jaw and the muscles of his cheeks, which seemed bunched in concentration, or perhaps pain. She did not think him a beggar, but neither did he appear to be a man of substance. The lone plodding mule and the cart with its solid wheels and its dusty wickerwork sides spoke of hard nights under the sky.

As he climbed down to them, foolish Nandor challenged him without asking her permission. "Hold, stranger, and state your business here." He squared his skinny shoulders. "These girls are under my protection." He glanced back to gauge Julianja's reaction.

While he was thus distracted, the knotted man cuffed the boy. It was just a glancing blow, but Nandor collapsed as if his bones had turned to noodles. "My business is none of yours," said the knotted man, "and my affairs are mine alone."

Nandor did not reply. His mouth was slack, eyes empty.

"Go." He hauled the boy upright and aimed him down the road. "This girl has no need of protection from me." The boy weaved away as if he had been drinking his father's *pálinka*.

The knotted man stepped to the garden gate. "She is dead then," he said. "Did many come to her garden after?"

"Some. Fewer than before."

"Where is she buried?"

"In a cave."

"Sealed?"

"With a boulder."

"How big?"

Julianja raised a hand over her head then spread her arms.

The knotted man grunted. "I was told there was a dark-haired girl who made the roses breathe."

"Vica. She grew up and was sent away."

"And you are?"

While Tzigana had shared precious little of her arts with her girls, she had impressed on them the charmed power of their true names. She was not about to give a stranger influence over her. "The rose girl," she said.

He seemed annoyed by her answer, but let it pass. "Already they are dying?" He reached out to snap one of the blackened twigs entwined in the fence. "Are there any left?"

Julianja was tired of his questions. She had some of her own. "My affairs are mine alone."

"Just so." His smile of acknowledgment was tight. "If you are the rose girl, then you can perform the charm. I've come from the castle of Kisvárda and crossed the Great Alföld to learn my future."

Julianja managed to conceal her excitement. No visitor had ever revealed his purpose before, at least, not to her. "I've never heard of this castle of yours, sir. Tzigana taught that entry here is a privilege." She bowed as if to dismiss him. "A shame to have travelled this far in vain."

He gripped the top of the gate so tight that it complained on its hinges. "What is it you want, rose girl?"

She paused to consider, for she couldn't remember anyone ever asking her such a question. "Answers."

The knots on his knuckles relaxed. "If I have them, they're yours."

She took his measure as she led him to the back of the garden. He was surely more than a boy but less than a man in full. He made a motley impression. His stride had resolve and confidence, and hard use had yet to stoop his shoulders. While his clothes were common, they were unusually clean for a traveler; there were no smears of mud on his leggings. He had the sweet scent of wood smoke about him, but not the stink of ancient sweat. Had he bathed and washed his clothes before arriving at the witch's garden? And what to make of the rough cart and the bony mule? He may well have come from a castle, although not one that prospered. She sensed an odd tension to him, like a rope that has been twisted too tight, or a sapling bent for a twitch snare.

They stopped by the cherry tree. "Only the dog rose is still blooming," she said.

"Good." He gazed up at the wild climber with its profusion of simple pink-tinged blossoms. "This is the one."

"You have been here before?"

"No. My father visited the year I was born. He's dead now, like your witch."

"So the castle is yours now?"

"I sleep beneath its walls." He laughed bitterly. "So do our goats. Castle Kisvárda has been a ruin since the reign of Mátyás the Just." Seeing her indignation at being misled, he held up a hand to beg patience. "It's mine, but my sad birthright includes a curse. My father said I might consult the roses to find out if I am the one to lift it."

Julianja couldn't decide if she should send him away or not. She'd never worked the charm on the dog rose because nobody had ever chosen it. Perhaps it waited for some eminence from even farther away than this pitiable traveler, someone who was even now on his way to her. "A curse?" she said.

"He was a man who was never easy in the wide world with its getting and spending. He was honorable, for all that, and came here to discover if it was his fate to lift our curse. He never said what he learned, but he came home a disappointed man."

"And now here you are. What do you expect to find out?"

"He called me to his deathbed, and told me that I should gather the family treasure and seek the fearsome witch Tzigana, as he had done in his time. He told me that I must convince her to let me pass into her garden, where a dark-haired girl would lead me to its humblest rose. There I must breathe its charmed breath. He told me what to expect after, although had he not been my own good father, I would have thought him mad. He claimed that in the instant he smelled this rose, all of his long life happened. He could see the inside of his mother's womb, the coffin he would lie in and everything in between. Each day of his past he lived again as well as all the days of his future, only outside of time. All and all. Perfect memory, perfect foresight. And so, he claimed, it would be for me. But I ask you, how can you remember something that hasn't yet happened? The Doctors of the Church teach that we have free will. How is that possible if our futures are already ordained?"

Fascinated as she was by this story, Julianja could not resist interrupting the knotted man. "You bring not only a curse, sir, but also a treasure?"

He shook his head. "A treasure in the same way that Kisvárda is a castle. It is of value only to my family." He waved towards the gate. "In my cart. I will show it to you after, if you like."

She tried to square this tale with the reactions of other visitors she had observed. The dowager and the bishop and the boar had come many times to the garden, and had never once seemed awed by their experience. Had they become jaded by the roses? "Aren't you afraid to know the future?"

"I am." The knotted man hooked the rope cinched around his waist and rolled it between thumb and forefinger. "But my father assured me that when time started for him again, the vision passed. Tzigana told him that no man's mind can hold his entire life at once, so he must ask himself one question while under the charm. The answer would be all that he clearly remembered. And so I will ask what I must do with the treasure."

"I thought you wanted to lift the curse."

"The treasure and the curse are one and the same." He noticed himself teasing the rope and let it fall. "So, I have given you the few answers I have, rose girl. Will you help me?"

You have very little understanding of the life of a girl at that time and in that place. You do not wake at the first hint of dawn or take to your bed at dusk because it is too dark to do anything else. You have never tried to eke a day's nourishment from an onion and some rotting parsnips or squatted over a cesspit. Julianja's life with Tzigana had presented her with precious few choices and all of those were predictable and circumscribed. She'd not even had the power to decide which chore to do first, whether to spend a dreary day sweeping dirt floors or scavenging firewood. Never had she had power over another—and a man, at that. His helplessness intoxicated her in a way she did not fully understand. Of course, she might have dismissed his plea. But then he would go and she would still be where she had always been and no longer wanted to be.

She reached for a stem and pinched it, impaling her forefinger. She blew her own red blood onto a blossom and nodded for him to approach.

The muscles of his jaw worked as he emptied his lungs, then he closed his eyes and pushed himself forward. He inhaled. Instantly his shoulders stiffened and his hands curled into fists and, with a shout, he was thrown backwards, arms windmilling. He sprawled at her feet, gibbering, and she dropped to her knees beside him. His eyes had rolled up. She grasped his tunic and rocked him from side to side, because he was too big for her to lift.

"Look at me, you. Look here."

He blinked. Groaned.

"Did you see your future?"

He stared at her.

"Do you remember any of it?"

He shivered.

"Did you ask the question?"

His mouth fell open and he tapped two fingers to his lower lip. Drink.

She fetched the bucket from the well. Soon he was sitting up. Although he could not speak, he would nod or shake his head in response to questions. She thought he might have been struck dumb, although she had never witnessed such a severe reaction to the charm. Did this mean that he was unworthy to smell the rose? Had she violated some magical law by giving him access to the charm? Perhaps the witch would rise from the tomb to exact a revenge. At that moment, all she wanted was to get him out of the garden and back on the road. For want of anything better, she brought him a cup of cold porridge to help him regain his strength.

She offered the ladle and he swallowed the gluey mess. His tongue flicked. "It's you."

"What is?"

"My future. The curse. The treasure. You."

Although she was certain he was wrong, the thought of escaping her life intrigued her. She wanted to know more, so when he was able to stand, she led him to his cart.

The mule grazed in the burdock at the side of the road. There was a mound of something in the cart, covered by hemp canvas treated with rosin against the weather. With eyes fixed on her, he pulled it aside. She caught her breath but did not otherwise react. Bones, so many bones, some the color of mushrooms, others gray as ash. Long femurs and delicate finger bones. Curved ribs, the bowl of a pelvis. A scatter of vertebrae and jaws with ragged arrays of teeth. She did not have to see the skulls to know that these were human remains. She counted two. Was that a third at the bottom of the pile?

"These are my ancestors," said the knotted man. "Wizards, if the tales we've been told are to be believed. Dead so long before my father's father's time that their names are lost. We call them the uncles. Their bones were entrusted to our care at the castle, but they do not rest. We believe they want peace, and until they get it, our lives are not our own."

"Cover them." The other girls might return at any time. "I've seen enough of your treasure."

He tugged the canvas into place. "The charm worked as my father said, although he never warned of the shock when it released me. I asked myself what the uncles wanted and I saw myself standing in the ruins of a church on a hill in the Badacsony overlooking Lake Balaton. With you."

"And I was doing what?"

"Nothing," he said. "Watching."

This was not the answer she wanted. "How do you know it's a true vision?"

"It's your charm, rose girl. I don't know how I know anything. I've never been to that place or to Lake Balaton. How did I know it was a ruined church? Where did I get the name Badacsony?" He rubbed his temples and grimaced. "But I saw you there."

"You could be lying."

He held out his hands, palms up, in surrender to her doubts. "Because I have seen what I have seen, I ask you now to come with me. But because there is no reason that you should, I'll take myself down the road and find a field to spend the night." He backed his mule between the shafts of the cart and tied ropes to its leather harness. "You may join me or not as you see fit." He spoke in a low voice, almost as if talking to himself. "Why should I try to convince you? If the vision was true, you'll be there. Perhaps you'll decide to make the journey by yourself."

He hauled himself onto the cart with a pained grunt. "I wanted none of this," he said, "but the uncles are restless and my life is not my own." He tapped his switch to the mule's withers and it gave a brief, scraping bray of protest. "In the morning I will be on my way."

One by one the girls returned to the witch's house that night. They dined merrily and well. Frici came home with a loaf of black bread that was only a day old, which she broke into eight chunks. Gyuri, the baker's son, was courting her with gifts of food, and now that Tzigana wasn't around to scare him off, he had become quite bold. Even better, Erzebet presented them with a cut of fatty pork the size of a fist, although she would not reveal how she had secured this prize. They boiled the pork with cabbage and Erzebet was declared the cleverest of them all. All Julianja had to contribute to the meal were the last radishes from the garden. She did not speak of Nandor or the knotted man as the other girls chattered about how Pisti's goat had got loose and wandered into the church or the boil on Father Vidor's nose or what mischief this boy and that boy and the other had gotten into. As usual, Julianja did not take part in their gossiping.

You know already how little experience she had making decisions. Propped on her straw pallet with a good round log for a bolster, she stared into the night long after everyone had fallen silent. She, who had unwittingly shown the future to so many others, had never imagined her own. Tzigana had been her future, her past and her present. But the witch was dead and her roses were dying, even as the dowager had predicted. What hold did this place have on her? You might say the companionship of the girls, but the truth was that they resented her for earning Tzigana's favor and she had little patience for them. Erzebet and Frici were already trysting with boys in the forest and would soon find their ways to beds in the village. Let the other girls spend the rest of their nights listening to Nandor and his lot snore. The witch's last charm linked her future to that of the knotted man. She should go with him. Must go. Afterwards, if there was no place for her in the wide world, she could always make him return her to Tzigana's house.

It took eight days for Julianja and the knotted man to reach the western shore of Lake Balaton. At first the roads were impossible, little more than dirt tracks that meandered through the forest, sometimes to emerge into a sunny field where stone-faced peasants watched them pass. Then they reached a town with a castle built on an old Roman road and began to make fifteen or twenty miles a day. This ancient thoroughfare had stood the test of time and traffic, except in the hamlets where pavers had been looted for buildings. Along the way they crossed innumerable rivers and streams, mostly at fords, sometimes on ferries and occasionally on a bridge.

The knotted man was a taciturn travelling companion. This suited Julianja, who was chary of his intent. They had yet to trust one another with their true names. At first he insisted that she ride on the cart while he walked beside, but soon she realized that they would make better progress if the mule were not pulling her weight. So she walked—usually on the opposite side of the cart from him—all the long day. When it rained, they got wet. When it didn't, they were hot. She wasn't sure which made her more uncomfortable. At dusk they would stop, gather wood for a fire, eat a simple dinner and then sleep under the cart.

The knotted man carried a purse that was fat with the king's own *denars*. Although he claimed this was all the money he had in the world, he spent freely on provisions along the way: bread and cheese and pottage if they were near a village, salt pork and pickled herring and dried fruit for when they stopped in the forest. Julianja had never eaten so well at Tzigana's. They drank no water, only small beer when it was available, or ale if it was not. She preferred the beer. Ale made her dizzy and then sleepy. The knotted man said she must never drink water while on the road, for the water of the country folk hated strangers and would loosen the bowels or light a fever in the unwary. Beer and ale were the traveler's true friends. A man could live a week on small beer alone. Casting sidelong glances at him as they walked, she decided that he must speak from knowledge of the road. She found herself wishing he would speak to her more often.

But one thing puzzled her. He didn't seem to be afraid, not of the beasts of the forest nor the brigands who lurked at every turning, if the stories were to be believed. He showed his purse as if it held only coppers. More than once she had noticed the hooded eyes of those who saw the glint of silver within its depths. The first time she asked about safeguards, he just shook his head. When she asked the second, he told her not to worry. It was not until she insisted that he told her that he and his family were protected by the uncles. Neither man nor beast nor force of nature could do them harm. This too was part of the treasure, he said, although not one that could be spent. "My father used to say that we should fear nothing, and expect nothing, which is why our treasure is also our curse. Once my family built a castle, but after decades tending the uncles, all that's left is a ruin. As long as they rule us, we may have no ambitions of our own. They keep us safe, but the price is that we can never grow and prosper."

She decided that the uncle's protection charm must be the reason that he gave himself over to regular acts of lunacy. She had witnessed one when they had forded a river on the second day but it was nothing like the time that he jumped off the ferry into the Duna.

And swam. She had heard tales of swimming, but had thought them absurd.

The knotted man would strip off all his clothes. She did not scruple to stare at his body, which was as muscular and knotted as she had imagined. And yes, she made note of his penis. She had seen the members of toddling boys in her village, but never before that of a man. It seemed at once so delicate and misshapen that she wondered at the stories the other girls had told of its power to enthrall. But her glimpse of his penis was over as soon as he hurled himself head first into the murderous water. On the ferry, the captain cried out in alarm and let go of the tiller. The oarsmen all rushed to the side to proffer oars, tilting the deck. The mule whickered. And still he did not emerge from the depths. When he did, sputtering, he'd laughed at their concern. It had been the only time she had seen him merry. To demonstrate his prowess, he kicked his legs, his arms stroked rhythmically, his head dipped in and out of the river, all perfectly coordinated. It struck Julianja as a kind of gliding, watery dance, horizontal instead of vertical.

"I thought you said to avoid water?" she called.

"I'm not drinking it," came his response. "I'm playing."

At that moment she stopped questioning her decision to accompany the knotted man. Imagine that you believe, as the learned alchemists and philosophers did, that everything consists of four elements: earth, air, fire and water. Common folk negotiate their passage across the earth as a matter of course. However, only angels frolic in the sky, while devils alone reside in fire. To Julianja, the knotted man's mastery of water as magical as any of the witch's charms.

On the eighth day, the Roman road veered south so they left it behind. Late that afternoon they reached the western shore of the lake. Inquiring at a farmhouse where they bought fresh eggs, root cellar carrots and dried catfish, the ale-wife told them the ruined church of the knotted man's vision was likely the *kolostor* of Mária Magdolna, near the village of Salföld on the eastern shore. A day's journey, perhaps longer with the cart.

She'd known that the knotted man had been growing more agitated as they traveled, but now Julianja realized how overwrought he was. At times the next day he would leave Julianja with the cart to forge ahead, as if he thought to show the mule how to pick up its pace. Eventually he would wait for them to catch up and glare, first at the plodding animal, then at her, as if they had betrayed his trust. He balked at stopping for a midday meal. Even so, as evening's shadows crept across the road, they could see that the hill on which the ruins stood was yet miles away. Reluctantly he diverted from the road to the shore of the lake to spend the night.

She built a fire and cooked the eggs while he paced the shore. There had been no small beer at the farmhouse and so they drank ale that was still fermenting with their meal. It was yeasty and sour and it settled in her belly like a stump. Afterwards she sat on a rock, mesmerized by the fire and the weight of the alcohol. The knotted man ceased his prowling and stripped.

"In the dark?" she said. "What should I do if something happens?"

"Fetch my corpse back to shore."

He marched into the glitter cast by the gibbous moon. The sweltering night air carried the sound of his splashing as he chased a wary mother duck and her brood. After a moment she rose and pulled off her shift. Threading through the grass along the shore, she put her toes into the water and gasped. The knotted man glanced back at her. Did he wave an encouragement? Hard to tell, since he was just a shadow in the moonlight. Then he dove and was lost to sight. She found the water cool but not unpleasant, especially since her cheeks were burning. She waded, mud squishing between her toes, until the water was just above her knees, then sat all at once. She gasped at the lusciousness of the sensation, then ran hands over her slippery legs, slicked the tight skin of her belly, rubbed the gooseflesh of her arms. She cupped water to her face, splashed her hair until it clung to her neck. The world felt cool and new, dark with promise. Then he was coming ashore so she leapt up. She had slithered into her tunic by the time he reached the grass.

He dressed, then noticed that she was shivering. "Now will you get sick on me?" He retrieved a small jug from the cart. "Drink this."

"What is it?"

"Tanglefoot." He offered it to her. "Spirits, distilled at the castle. Take a big swallow."

A gulp led to a fit of coughing. She might as well have breathed fire. "Again," he said.

He swigged from the jug himself as Julianja slumped onto her stone. Her body felt numb, but her mind was racing. "I don't know your name," she said.

He squatted beside her and gazed into the flames. "Miklos."

She repeated it, savored the taste of it on her tongue, decided she liked it. "Miklos." When she reached out toward him, he pretended not to notice. "How long does it take to dry, Miklos?" She touched the tight bundle of hair atop his head.

He started. "What did you say?"

"Your hair."

He studied her. She was sure that he hadn't paid this close attention since the day they had met.

"You should let it down," she said. "It'll dry faster." As if to illustrate she shook her head back and forth and giggled as wet strands slapped at her face. "See?"

The expression on his face—was he puzzled? Alarmed? She laughed to get a response after so many miles of silence. With hands on either side of her head she sifted her wet locks between her fingers and held her hair out in two wings. "Like this."

He considered and then, like a man caught in a dream, reached to the top knot and removed a silver pin, which he took between his teeth. He had divided a long ponytail into two halves and coiled them, one around the other. Eyes raised as if he could see the crown of his head, he now unwound each half. He dipped his head and they fell over his face, reunited into one long braid of hair splayed by gravity. She saw that it was held in place at the scalp by a ribbon of the same silk as the scarf he had worn that first day. She hadn't seen the scarf since they crossed Duna. What did that mean? She didn't know what anything meant anymore as he untied the ribbon and his dark, heavy hair came loose. His hands fell to his sides and he let the ribbon slip to the ground. She leaned close, parted the hair from in front of his eyes and sifted it between her fingers. She spread it into wet wings. Neither of them laughed.

"It is good this way," she said. "I think so."

He took the pin from his mouth and set it beside the ribbon. "What is your name, rose girl?" he said.

"Julianja," she whispered.

The mad tremolo of a loon made them aware of how close they were. Embarrassed, they pulled back from the moment and one another. Miklos threw some sticks on the fire. She watched as if this were a skill she must learn.

"You say you have a family, Miklos?"

"My widowed mother. A younger brother."

"No wife?"

"I am not permitted." His eyes glittered in the firelight. "Perhaps after tomorrow."

"And what will happen tomorrow?"

Miklos thought for a moment, then gave a bitter chuckle. "Only tomorrow knows." He rose and walked away from the fire without bidding her good night.

If you do not understand Julianja, know that she did not understand herself either. And who can blame her? She was a girl who had never been farther from home than a day's walk, who had never drunk tanglefoot or seen a man naked. She was a girl who had set her life aside to follow a cursed stranger on a quest that he could not—or would not—explain. What gave her the right to do this? She didn't know exactly, but she believed that she had that right. It had something to do with the witch choosing her to work the charm in the garden. Dorottya had wanted to care for the roses, and she was the eldest. Erzebet had begged to be chosen and she was the prettiest. And yet it had been Julianja who had greeted Miklos when he'd come to the gate. Why? Maybe because when the other girls worked one of Tzigana's charms, they said a witch's prayer or rubbed a talisman. The charm was not in them the way it was in her. In Julianja's blood. Julianja was the charm. Julianja was magic. Tanglefooted thoughts began to trip one another into drowsy darkness. Just before sleep came, she realized something important, although she would not remember it in the morning.

The reason Miklos did not stink like every other man she had ever met was that he liked to swim.

It took several hours to coax the mule up the steep track to the ruined *kolostor*. Lush summer growth of silkybent and ragweed and goose grass brushed against the bottom of the cart. From time to time, Miklos got behind to push. They found the ruins in a wood where saplings encroached on snaggle-toothed foundations. Deadwood leaned against the forlorn stone and mortar walls of buildings that had long since lost roofs. Miklos tethered the mule to graze and they split up to explore. Most of the valuables the monks had hoarded were gone, even some of the stone carvings had been carried off. Julianja kicked at a midden of shattered glass and pots in what she guessed was the refectory. All around her the buzz and chirp and hum of the natural world mocked the fleeting works of men. Just beyond the ruined wall a musk rose had returned to the wild, its unsupported canes bent to the ground. Most of the stems had gone to rose hips but there was one last spray of pink tinged blossoms. When Julianja lifted the flowers to her nose to smell, she pricked her finger. She stared at the bead of blood in surprise. She could feel her future closing in around her.

"Julianja!"

The western wall of the church had collapsed. The row of eight empty lancet windows on the eastern wall hinted at the lost wealth of the monastery. Much of the plaster on this wall had peeled away, revealing the rough stone beneath. But Julianja could make out a few murals, paint faded by weather. The sorrowful eyes of Christ watched as she made her way down the nave and the draped arm of a woman, perhaps the Magdalen reached out to her.

Miklos waited in the chancel, face flushed, eyes wild. "Here," He stood on the altar, a broken slab of marble overthrown from a limestone pedestal. "In my vision I saw the bones here."

They stripped away the hemp canvas that covered the bones and spread it beside the cart. They carried the treasure to the church in three trips. Miklos had no way to tell which bones belonged to which uncle, but, as a gesture of respect, he set just one skull and two halves of a pelvis in each of the bone piles they arranged before the altar. Then he fetched the skin of water he had filled at the lake that morning, poured it into a wooden bucket and produced the missing silk scarf. He explained that now he must wash the bones.

"Then what?"

"Then we will see if my father spoke truly." He knelt, retrieved a heavy leg bone, dipped the scarf into the water, braced himself, and daubed gingerly at the knob end, as he was expecting it to twist from his grip or burst into flame. When nothing happened, he washed the bone and then placed it next to the pile from which he had retrieved it. He leaned back, waiting for some reaction. None came. He found another bone, dipped the scarf and washed. This bone he set atop the first. Nothing happened.

"May I help?" Julianja touched his shoulder.

He shook her off without looking up. He sorted through the pile, found the skull and held it, gazing for a moment at the empty eye sockets. Then he scrubbed as if it were a dirty cook pot. Finally satisfied, he tried to balance it on the two bones in the new pile. As soon as he withdrew his hand, it toppled onto its side, staring up at them in mute reproach.

"Must be all in all," Miklos muttered.

"Let me help." She hovered over him.

"*No.*" He pointed the jagged end of a broken femur at her and she backed away. "When I saw this in your garden, you were here but you only watched."

He continued his task with flagging enthusiasm. He finished the first pile and scooted across the dirty floor of the chancel on his knees to the second. He worked faster now, carelessly. She saw him gather a knot of finger bones, give them a single swipe and toss them onto the second pile. He seemed resigned, like a man forced to play out his part in some humiliating practical joke.

As he washed, Julianja counted the bones to herself. Keeping a tally of his progress seemed like a kind of support, the only kind he would permit.

"*A kurva életbe*!" Finally he hurled the filthy scarf at the pile, picked up an armful of unwashed bones, stood and let them drop, one by one, to bounce and scatter.

"Miklos!"

"The bones do not dance." He spun away from her, eyes red, cheeks wet. "My father promised they would dance. I've done everything I'm supposed to do, everything I can do." He shoulders sagged. "For nothing."

Seeing him so reduced filled Julianja with terror and pity and, yes, anger. She'd believed they would arrive safely at this place because he claimed to know the ways of the wide world. She'd trusted what he'd told her of his future. After all, hadn't she herself shown it to him? But he'd deceived her—and probably himself. She realized he'd never told her that he had actually witnessed the lifting of the curse, only that she would be there when he tried. Seeing him now, defeated and unmanned, brought all her doubts back. And yet she wanted to help, if only because it was in her power. Julianja *was* powerful, in the same way the Tzigana had been. She was as certain of this as she was of the breath that swelled her lungs, the blood that pounded in her chest. When she bent to retrieve the scarf, it was like falling, at once inevitable and frightening. She picked a skull that poor Miklos had already washed and dipped the scarf into the bucket. As her hand touched water, she felt the finger she had pricked on the musk rose start to throb. A pink stain swirled in the clear water.

"But you just watched," cried Miklos. "Watched only."

The cold bone seemed to suck the warmth from the palm of her hand. Perhaps Miklos had experienced a true vision, but he had not seen all. When she swiped its brow, the skull blinked and gazed at her with milky, ghost eyes. She wanted to scream, but her throat closed with fear. Instead she turned his uncle's terrible gaze on Miklos, who fell away as if she were showing him his death.

"Look," she whispered.

All it took was a touch of the damp silk. Julianja might have called what the bones did a dance, although it was more like the rolling and tumbling of maggots. They would find their proper alignment and knit together. Watching them gather themselves made her feel unsure of her footing. It was as if the earth itself was twitching. First, one, then another, then all three uncles stood before them. But the uncles were no longer ghastly skeletons. A sinuous, indistinct glow suffused the bones, first as the flesh of transfigured, luminous bodies, then as the finery you might have seen at the Mátyás Palace in Buda. The shimmer of these magical creatures reminded Julianja of the way her legs had looked beneath the ripples of Lake Balaton.

One was dressed in an antique red cap with a feather, black velvet breeches and a red leather doublet with golden buttons. The second wore a green tunic embroidered with gold thread under a surcoat of silk so fine that it might have been spun from emeralds. The last wore a robe of midnight blue trimmed with ermine. Around his neck hung a heavy gold chain from which depended a brooch in the shape of a scroll inlaid with letters of lapis lazuli. All three uncles bore a resemblance to Miklos, although each was distinct. The red uncle was a jaunty rake who gave Julianja a sly look that made her flush. The green was older, more kindly, a man of substance whom she felt she might trust. She imagined that the solemn blue uncle, the eldest, had judged her at a glance and found her wanting.

"You have served our family well, Miklos Kemény." The green uncle stretched, as if waking from a nap and not from the dead.

The blue was as impassive as an owl. "Much better than your father Miklos or his father Benci or his father Benedek, or his father Ambrus, who was the son of Lajos Kemény, our own dear brother."

The red winked at Julianja. "No one of your line ever thought to bring us a beautiful witch."

"I am not a witch," said Julianja. But the words seemed to twist on her tongue. After all, hadn't her blood just brought the three uncles back to the world of the living? Hadn't she felt the stirring of her powers last night at the lake?

"Yet you are clearly the one we have been waiting for," said the green. "What is your name, child?"

Julianja stiffened. She felt the uncles seeking to sway her. But why? They were Miklos's ancestors. This was his quest.

The blue uncle scowled at her. "Say it!"

"Julianja," said Miklos. "Her name is Julianja. What does it matter, her name, if the curse is lifted?"

"Come close, *Julianja.*" The red uncle crooked his finger and it was as if he had tugged at a tether around her waist. "You have done our family a great service, but there is something yet we must ask of you."

The green gave her his gentle smile. "Know that, in life, we three brothers cast a charm so that we would not pass completely from this world when our bodies failed. The nature of that charm was such that we could exist between life and death in a place of our devising."

"We realize now that was a trap," said the blue, "and we have chosen you to help us escape it. We bind you by your name to choose a spouse this day. Whomever you chose will return to full life. The others will pass on." He glared at his brothers as if daring them to differ. "We are so agreed."

"What is this?" Miklos pushed past to confront the uncles. "What of the curse, of me and my family?"

The red uncle looked bored. "You have done well, Miklos son of Miklos."

"Yes, I have," he cried. "I have done all . . . "

The blue held out his hand, palm facing Miklos, who immediately fell silent, although the muscles of his jaw worked as he struggled to speak. The uncle rotated his hand, palm upward, and flicked it twice toward the sky. Miklos lifted off the ground a few inches, dangling like laundry from a branch. He twisted frantically against invisible knots until the blue uncle closed his fist and he sagged into unconsciousness.

Sensing Julianja's outrage at this ill treatment, the green uncle apologized. "We understand why he is angry, but there is still much to explain and little time. Don't be afraid, we won't harm him. He is of us, a Kemény."

"I'm not afraid," said Julianja, and was pleased to discover that this was true. "But neither am I impressed by the way you treat those who help you."

"You may be right. Perhaps we have been too long away from the world." The green spoke to her, but she guessed that he was also chiding his blue brother.

"Only choose," said the blue, "and we will be done with curses."

"Choose," agreed the red.

"Yes, choose." The green opened his arms wide, as if to embrace her.

She straightened, threw back her shoulders and found the inner strength to defy them, for all their magical power. "And what if I do not? Will you compel me?"

"You mistake us, Julianja." The blue seemed offended. "We would not compel such a decision."

Red laughed. "We would rather entice you."

"For such a woman as you," said the green, "the bride price would be very high indeed."

You will understand why this would give Julianja pause, as a penniless orphan who was many days journey away from a household that might not welcome her return. She tried not to show her interest. "I would hear more," she said.

The red spoke first. "Choose me so that I may fill your senses to overflowing. In this world that men have made, there is precious little room for a woman's pleasure. You will blush at the thought, but I will lead you to a new world, where desire never wanes and cries of ecstasy fill the long night. You will never grow weary of love, nor bored of our marriage bed, for I will be a student of your body, so that I may learn all that you secretly crave but know not how to ask for. I will be all men to you and any man you fancy. This is within my power to offer you, Julianja, for all the days of your life."

As she listened her cheeks burned and she imagined bare legs entwined, strong arms enfolding her, her blood shouting so that it drowned out all thought. She remembered then what Erzebet had whispered to her about the power of love, and understood for the first time.

The green bowed to her then. "My brother speaks truly. But the world he offers is a small world indeed. You have five senses, yes, but we are more than our senses. Choose me and together we will make a place in the world beyond the bedroom door. I will comfort and support you, and keep you forever safe from evil. Our friends will love us and strangers will admire us. You will be proud of all we accomplish together. Oh, and our beautiful children! I will be the father to them that every mother hopes for. I will cherish and nurture them so that they will prosper and bring joy to us. We will get kings and philosophers! This is within my power to offer you, Julianja, for all the days of your life."

This future she knew, was no trick of imagination. She looked into the green's smiling eyes and saw a great house, a long table laden with joints of meat and exotic fruit. Silver plate, crystal goblets and raven-haired children laughing, as she would laugh and laugh as she told them of her impoverished years with Tzigana. Julianja thought then of Dorottya, struggling to hold the dead witch's household together.

The blue regarded her sternly. "My brothers speak the truth. Do not doubt their promises, but consider what I alone offer you. You have a talent that must be expressed, or you will surely live a life of regret. You deny that you are a witch. But witch is a word that men call women who have powers they do not understand. Powers they fear. I will help you understand who you are, discover what your unique abilities might be and what they can accomplish. Pleasure and the regard of others will only distract you from the task of knowing yourself, which is our true life's work. I can show you the greatness which seethes within you. Don't throw away this chance, Julianja, or you will rue what you've lost all the days of your life."

This speech frightened her, for she knew already that she was powerful. She could only guess what she might be capable of. The blue expected more from her than she expected from herself. She wasn't sure that she wanted this greatness he spoke of, even if it did dwell within her. Had Tzigana made a similar choice to perfect her abilities? If so, Julianja had witnessed its cost. She had been powerful, but never happy.

And yet, as tempting as each of these offers was in its own way, the manner in which they were being offered annoyed her. The uncles were so confident that what they proposed was what she must want. "Why must I chose any of you?" She stamped her foot. "What if I want all of what you offer? Or none of it? And if I do chose, why should it be one of you? Why shouldn't I choose him?" She turned to gesture at the slumbering Miklos. At least he was a man of honest flesh and blood, not a construct of bones and dark magic.

The red uncle sneered in disbelief. The blue uncle shook his head sadly. Only the green uncle pleaded with her. "Would you really choose an ordinary life, when we can make dreams real? He may be a good man, but what he can give you is just the smallest part of what we offer."

"Nevertheless . . . " she said, but when she turned back to them she found that she had chosen, as so many of us do, without meaning to. Was it because she refused to embrace their choices and had argued with them? Or because she truly wanted Miklos? No matter. In the flicker of indecision, the moment passed. The uncles were gone and in their places were three sorry mounds of dust.

Miklos groaned and slumped to the floor of the chancel.

You may ask, what happened next? That evening and the next morning and ever after? You may wonder, as Julianja did, whether she was bound by the charm of the uncles. Since she had thwarted them, she believed she was not. She considered the unconscious Miklos, whom she had freed from his family curse. Should she now accompany him to the castle of Kisvárda? And if she did, would she ever understand why?

Recall what Tzigana told Miklos, father of Miklos, back when that brave and disappointed man ventured into her garden. No one's mind can hold an entire life at once. But believe this: Julianja would think about that summer afternoon for years to come. Not every day, but on occasion. Because, like all of us, there would be times when she was frustrated with her life, when she could not help but imagine what might have been.

And yet there is one last thing for you to know. Before she went to awaken Miklos from his trance, before she decided what she would do with him, Julianja overturned his leaky bucket. The pink-tinged water she had used to wake the bones spilled down the broken altar stone and darkened the thirsty earth. She carried the bucket to the piles of dust, knelt and scooped three handfuls from each into it. As she did this, she vowed to the witch Tzigana, Mária Magdolna and the Blessed Virgin that someday she would scatter the treasure of the Kemény onto the roses in a charmed garden that would be hers, and hers alone.

ABOUT THE AUTHOR

James Patrick Kelly made his first sale in 1975, and since has gone on to become one of the most respected and popular writers to enter the field in the last twenty years. Although Kelly has had some success with novels, he has perhaps had more impact to date as a writer of short fiction, and is often ranked among the best short story writers in the business. His story "Think Like a Dinosaur" won him a Hugo Award in 1996, as did his story "10^16 to 1," in 2000. Kelly's first solo novel, *Planet of Whispers,* came out in 1984. It was followed by *Freedom Beach,* a mosaic novel written in collaboration with John Kessel, and then by the solo novels, *Look Into the Sun and Wildside,* as well as the chapbook novella, *Burn.* His short work has been collected in *Think Like a Dinosaur* and *Strange But Not a Stranger.* His most recent book are a series of anthologies co-edited with John Kessel: *Feeling Very Strange: The Slipstream Anthology, The Secret History of Science Fiction, Digital Rapture: The Singularity Anthology, Rewired: The Post-Cyberpunk Anthology,* and *Nebula Awards Showcase 2012.* Born in Minneola, New York, Kelly now lives with his family in Nottingham, New Hampshire.

Seven Years from Home
NAOMI NOVIK

Preface

Seven days passed for me on my little raft of a ship as I fled Melida; seven years for the rest of the unaccelerated universe. I hoped to be forgotten, a dusty footnote left at the bottom of a page. Instead I came off to trumpets and medals and legal charges, equal doses of acclaim and venom, and I stumbled bewildered through the brassy noise, led first by one and then by another, while my last opportunity to enter any protest against myself escaped.

Now I desire only to correct the worst of the factual inaccuracies bandied about, so far as my imperfect memory will allow, and to make an offering of my own understanding to that smaller and more sophisticate audience who prefer to shape the world's opinion rather than be shaped by it.

I engage not to tire you with a recitation of dates and events and quotations. I do not recall them with any precision myself. But I must warn you that neither have I succumbed to that pathetic and otiose impulse to sanitize the events of the war, or to excuse sins either my own or belonging to others. To do so would be a lie, and on Melida, to tell a lie was an insult more profound than murder.

I will not see my sisters again, whom I loved. Here we say that one who takes the long midnight voyage has leaped ahead in time, but to me it seems it is they who have traveled on ahead. I can no longer hear their voices when I am awake. I hope this will silence them in the night.

Ruth Patrona
Reivaldt, Janvier 32, 4765

The First Adjustment

I disembarked at the port of Landfall in the fifth month of 4753. There is such a port on every world where the Confederacy has set its foot but not yet its flag: crowded and dirty and charmless. It was on the Esperigan continent, as the Melidans would not tolerate the construction of a spaceport in their own territory.

Ambassador Kostas, my superior, was a man of great authority and presence, two meters tall and solidly built, with a jovial handshake, high intelligence, and very little patience for fools; that I was likely to be relegated to this category was evident on our first meeting. He disliked my assignment to begin with. He thought well of the Esperigans; he moved in their society as easily as he did in our own, and would have called one or two of their senior ministers his personal friends, if only such a gesture were not highly unprofessional. He recognized his duty, and on an abstract intellectual level the potential value of the Melidans, but they revolted him, and he would have been glad to find me of like mind, ready to draw a line through their name and give them up as a bad cause.

A few moments' conversation was sufficient to disabuse him of this hope. I wish to attest that he did not allow the disappointment to in any way alter the performance of his duty, and he could not have objected with more vigor to my project of proceeding at once to the Melidan continent, to his mind a suicidal act.

In the end he chose not to stop me. I am sorry if he later regretted that, as seems likely. I took full advantage of the weight of my arrival. Five years had gone by on my homeworld of Terce since I had embarked, and there is a certain moral force to having sacrificed a former life for the one unknown. I had observed it often with new arrivals on Terce: their first requests were rarely refused even when foolish, as they often were. I was of course quite sure my own were eminently sensible.

"We will find you a guide," he said finally, yielding, and all the machinery of the Confederacy began to turn to my desire, a heady sensation.

Badea arrived at the embassy not two hours later. She wore a plain gray wrap around her shoulders, draped to the ground, and another wrap around her head. The alterations visible were only small ones: a smattering of green freckles across the bridge of her nose and cheeks, a greenish tinge to her lips and nails. Her wings were folded and hidden under the wrap, adding the bulk roughly of an overnight hiker's backpack. She smelled a little like the sourdough used on Terce to make roundbread, noticeable but not unpleasant. She might have walked through a spaceport without exciting comment.

She was brought to me in the shambles of my new office, where I had barely begun to lay out my things. I was wearing a conservative black suit, my best, tailored because you could not buy trousers for women ready-made on Terce, and, thankfully, comfortable shoes, because elegant ones on Terce were not meant to be walked in. I remember my clothing particularly because I was in it for the next week without opportunity to change.

"Are you ready to go?" she asked me, as soon as we were introduced and the receptionist had left.

I was quite visibly *not* ready to go, but this was not a misunderstanding: she did not want to take me. She thought the request stupid, and feared my safety would be a burden on her. If Ambassador Kostas would not mind my failure to return, she could not know that, and to be just, he would certainly have reacted unpleasantly in any case, figuring it as his duty.

But when asked for a favor she does not want to grant, a Melidan will sometimes offer it anyway, only in an unacceptable or awkward way. Another Melidan will recognize this as a refusal, and withdraw the request. Badea did not expect this courtesy from me, she only expected that I would say I could not leave at once. This she could count to her satisfaction as a refusal, and she would not come back to offer again.

I was however informed enough to be dangerous, and I did recognize the custom. I said, "It is inconvenient, but I am prepared to leave immediately." She turned at once and walked out of my office, and I followed her. It is understood that a favor accepted despite the difficulty and constraints laid down by the giver must be necessary to the recipient, as indeed this was to me; but in such a case, the conditions must then be endured, even if artificial.

I did not risk a pause at all even to tell anyone I was going; we walked out past the embassy secretary and the guards, who did not do more than give us a cursory glance—we were going the wrong way, and my citizen's button would likely have saved us interruption in any case. Kostas would not know I had gone until my absence was noticed and the security logs examined.

The Second Adjustment

I was not unhappy as I followed Badea through the city. A little discomfort was nothing to me next to the intense satisfaction of, as I felt, having passed a first test: I had gotten past all resistance offered me, both by Kostas and Badea, and soon I would be in the heart of a people I already felt I knew. Though I would be an outsider among them, I had lived all my life to the present day in the self-same state, and I did not fear it, or for the moment anything else.

Badea walked quickly and with a freer stride than I was used to, loose-limbed. I was taller, but had to stretch to match her. Esperigans looked at her as she went by, and then looked at me, and the pressure of their gaze was suddenly hostile. "We might take a taxi," I offered. Many were passing by empty. "I can pay."

"No," she said, with a look of distaste at one of those conveyances, so we continued on foot.

After Melida, during my black-sea journey, my doctoral dissertation on the Canaan movement was published under the escrow clause, against my will. I have never used the funds, which continue to accumulate steadily. I do not like to inflict them on any cause I admire sufficiently to support, so they will go to my family when I have gone; my nephews will be glad of it, and of the passing of an embarrassment, and that is as much good as it can be expected to provide.

There is a great deal within that book which is wrong, and more which is wrongheaded, in particular any expression of opinion or analysis I interjected atop the scant collection of accurate facts I was able to accumulate in six years of over-enthusiastic graduate work. This little is true: the Canaan movement was an offshoot of conservation philosophy. Where the traditionalists of that movement sought to restrict humanity to dead worlds and closed enclaves on others, the Canaan splinter group wished instead to alter themselves while they altered their new worlds, meeting them halfway.

The philosophy had the benefit of a certain practicality, as genetic engineering and body modification was and remains considerably cheaper than terraforming, but we are a squeamish and a violent species, and nothing invites pogrom more surely than the neighbor who is different from us, yet still too close. In consequence, the Melidans were by our present day the last surviving Canaan society.

They had come to Melida and settled the larger of the two continents some eight hundred years before. The Esperigans came two hundred years later, refugees from the plagues on New Victoire, and took the smaller continent. The two had little contact for the first half-millennium; we of the Confederacy are given to think in worlds and solar systems, and to imagine that only a space voyage is long, but a hostile continent is vast enough to occupy a small and struggling band. But both prospered, each according to their lights, and by the time I landed, half the planet glittered in the night from space, and half was yet pristine.

In my dissertation, I described the ensuing conflict as natural, which is fair if slaughter and pillage are granted to be natural to our kind. The Esperigans had exhausted the limited raw resources of their share of the planet, and a short flight away was the untouched expanse of the larger continent, not a tenth as populated as their own. The Melidans controlled their birthrate, used only sustainable quantities, and built nothing which could not be eaten by the wilderness a year after they had abandoned it. Many Esperigan philosophes and politicians trumpeted their admiration of Melidan society, but this was only a sort of pleasant spiritual refreshment, as one admires a saint or a martyr without ever wishing to be one.

The invasion began informally, with adventurers and entrepreneurs, with the desperate, the poor, the violent. They began to land on the shores of the Melidan territory, to survey, to take away samples, to plant their own foreign roots. They soon had a village, then more than one. The Melidans told them to leave, which worked as well as it ever has in the annals of colonialism, and then attacked them. Most of the settlers were killed; enough survived and straggled back across the ocean to make a dramatic story of murder and cruelty out of it.

I expressed the conviction to the Ministry of State, in my pre-assignment report, that the details had been exaggerated, and that the attacks had been provoked more extensively. I was wrong, of course. But at the time I did not know it.

Badea took me to the low quarter of Landfall, so called because it faced on the side of the ocean downcurrent from the spaceport. Iridescent oil and a floating mat of discards glazed the edge of the surf. The houses were mean and crowded tightly upon one another, broken up mostly by liquor stores and bars. Docks stretched out into the ocean, extended long to reach out past the pollution, and just past the end of one of these floated a small boat, little more than a simple coracle: a hull of brown bark, a narrow brown mast, a grey-green sail slack and trembling in the wind.

We began walking out towards it, and those watching—there were some men loitering about the docks, fishing idly, or working on repairs to equipment or nets—began to realize then that I meant to go with her.

The Esperigans had already learned the lesson we like to teach as often as we can, that the Confederacy is a bad enemy and a good friend, and while no one is ever made to join us by force, we cannot be opposed directly. We had given them the spaceport already, an open door to the rest of the settled worlds, and they wanted more, the moth yearning. I relied on this for protection, and did not consider that however much they wanted from our outstretched hand, they still more wished to deny its gifts to their enemy.

Four men rose as we walked the length of the dock, and made a line across it. "You don't want to go with that one, ma'am," one of them said to me, a parody of respect. Badea said nothing. She moved a little aside, to see how I would answer them.

"I am on assignment for my government," I said, neatly offering a red flag to a bull, and moved towards them. It was not an attempt at bluffing: on Terce, even though I was immodestly unveiled, men would have at once moved out of the way to avoid any chance of the insult of physical contact. It was an act so automatic as to be invisible: precisely what we are taught to watch for in ourselves, but that proves infinitely easier in the instruction than in the practice. I did not *think* they would move; I knew they would.

Perhaps that certainty transmitted itself: the men did move a little, enough to satisfy my unconscious that they were cooperating with my expectations, so that it took me wholly by surprise and horror when one reached out and put his hand on my arm to stop me.

I screamed, in full voice, and struck him. His face is lost to my memory, but I still can see clearly the man behind him, his expression as full of appalled violation as my own. The four of them flinched from my scream, and then drew in around me, protesting and reaching out in turn.

I reacted with more violence. I had confidently considered myself a citizen of no world and of many, trained out of assumptions and unaffected by the parochial attitudes of the one where chance had seen me born, but in that moment I could with actual pleasure have killed all of them. That wish was unlikely to be gratified. I was taller, and the gravity of Terce is slightly higher than of Melida, so I was stronger than they expected me to be, but they were laborers and seamen, built generously and rough-hewn, and the male advantage in muscle mass tells quickly in a hand-to-hand fight.

They tried to immobilize me, which only panicked me further. The mind curls in on itself in such a moment; I remember palpably only the sensation of sweating copiously, and the way this caused the seam of my blouse to rub unpleasantly against my neck as I struggled.

Badea told me later that, at first, she had meant to let them hold me. She could then leave, with the added satisfaction of knowing the Esperigan fishermen and not she had provoked an incident with the Confederacy. It was not sympathy that moved her to action, precisely. The extremity of my distress was as alien to her as to them, but where they thought me mad, she read it in the context of my having accepted her original conditions and somewhat unwillingly decided that I truly did need to go with her, even if she did not know precisely why and saw no use in it herself.

I cannot tell you precisely how the subsequent moments unfolded. I remember the green gauze of her wings overhead perforated by the sun, like a linen curtain, and the blood spattering my face as she neatly lopped off the hands upon me. She used for the purpose a blade I later saw in use for many tasks, among them harvesting fruit off plants where the leaves or the bark may be poisonous. It is shaped like a sickle and strung upon a thick elastic cord, which a skilled wielder can cause to become rigid or to collapse.

I stood myself back on my feet panting, and she landed. The men were on their knees screaming, and others were running towards us down the docks. Badea swept the severed hands into the water with the side of her foot and said calmly, "We must go."

The little boat had drawn up directly beside us over the course of our encounter, drawn by some signal I had not seen her transmit. I stepped into it behind her. The coracle leapt forward like a springing bird, and left the shouting and the blood behind.

We did not speak over the course of that strange journey. What I had thought a sail did not catch the wind, but opened itself wide and stretched out over our heads, like an awning, and angled itself towards the sun. There were many small filaments upon the surface wriggling when I examined it more closely, and also upon the exterior of the hull. Badea stretched herself out upon the floor of the craft, lying under the low deck, and I joined her in the small space: it was not uncomfortable nor rigid, but had the queer unsettled cushioning of a waterbed.

The ocean crossing took only the rest of the day. How our speed was generated I cannot tell you; we did not seem to sit deeply in the water and our craft threw up no spray. The world blurred as a window running with rain. I asked Badea for water, once, and she put her hands on the floor of the craft and pressed down: in the depression she made, a small clear pool gathered for me to cup out, with a taste like slices of cucumber with the skin still upon them.

This was how I came to Melida.

The Third Adjustment

Badea was vaguely embarrassed to have inflicted me on her fellows, and having deposited me in the center of her village made a point of leaving me there by leaping aloft into the canopy where I could not follow, as a way of saying she was done with me, and anything I did henceforth could not be laid at her door.

I was by now hungry and nearly sick with exhaustion. Those who have not flown between worlds like to imagine the journey a glamorous one, but at least for minor bureaucrats, it is no more pleasant than any form of transport, only elongated. I had spent a week a virtual prisoner in my berth, the bed folding up to give me room to walk four strides back and forth, or to unfold my writing desk, not both at once, with a shared toilet the size of an ungenerous closet down the hall. Landfall had not arrested my forward motion, as that mean port had never been my destination. Now, however, I was arrived, and the dregs of adrenaline were consumed in anticlimax.

Others before me have stood in a Melidan village center and described it for an audience—Esperigans mostly, anthropologists and students of biology and a class of tourists either adventurous or stupid. There is usually a lyrical description of the natives coasting overhead among some sort of vines or tree-branches knitted overhead for shelter, the particulars and adjectives determined by the village latitude, and the obligatory explanation of the typical plan of huts, organized as a spoked wheel around the central plaza.

If I had been less tired, perhaps I too would have looked with so analytical an air, and might now satisfy my readers with a similar report. But to me the village only presented all the confusion of a wholly strange place, and I saw nothing that seemed to me deliberate. To call it a village gives a false air of comforting provinciality. Melidans, at least those with wings, move freely among a wide constellation of small settlements, so that all of these, in the public sphere, partake of the hectic pace of the city. I stood alone, and strangers moved past me with assurance, the confidence of their stride saying, "I care nothing for you or your fate. It is of no concern to me. How might you expect it to be otherwise?" In the end, I lay down on one side of the plaza and went to sleep.

I met Kitia the next morning. She woke me by prodding me with a twig, experimentally, having been selected for this task out of her group of schoolmates by some complicated interworking of personality and chance. They giggled from a few safe paces back as I opened my eyes and sat up.

"Why are you sleeping in the square?" Kitia asked me, to a burst of fresh giggles.

"Where should I sleep?" I asked her.

"In a house!" she said.

When I had explained to them, not without some art, that I had no house here, they offered the censorious suggestion that I should go back to wherever I did have a house. I made a good show of looking analytically up at the sky overhead and asking them what our latitude was, and then I pointed at a random location and said, "My house is five years that way."

Scorn, puzzlement, and at last delight. I was from the stars! None of their friends had ever met anyone from so far away. One girl who previously had held a point of pride for having once visited the smaller continent, with an Esperigan toy doll to prove it, was instantly dethroned. Kitia possessively took my arm and informed me that as my house was too far away, she would take me to another.

Children of virtually any society are an excellent resource for the diplomatic servant or the anthropologist, if contact with them can be made without giving offense. They enjoy the unfamiliar experience of answering real questions, particularly the stupidly obvious ones that allow them to feel a sense of superiority over the inquiring adult, and they are easily impressed with the unusual. Kitia was a treasure. She led me, at the head of a small pied-piper procession, to an empty house on a convenient lane. It had been lately abandoned, and was already being reclaimed: the walls and floor were swarming with tiny insects with glossy dark blue carapaces, munching so industriously the sound of their jaws hummed like a summer afternoon.

I with difficulty avoided recoiling. Kitia did not hesitate: she walked into the swarm, crushing beetles by the dozens underfoot, and went to a small spigot in the far wall. When she turned this on, a clear viscous liquid issued forth, and the beetles scattered from it. "Here, like this," she said, showing me how to cup my hands under the liquid and spread it upon the walls and the floor. The disgruntled beetles withdrew, and the brownish surfaces began to bloom back to pale green, repairing the holes.

Over the course of that next week, she also fed me, corrected my manners and my grammar, and eventually brought me a set of clothing, a tunic and leggings, which she proudly informed me she had made herself in class. I thanked her with real sincerity and asked where I might wash my old clothing. She looked very puzzled, and when she had looked more closely at my clothing and touched it, she said, "Your clothing is dead! I thought it was only ugly."

Her gift was not made of fabric but a thin tough mesh of plant filaments with the feathered surface of a moth's wings. It gripped my skin eagerly as soon as I had put it on, and I thought myself at first allergic, because it itched and tingled, but this was only the bacteria bred to live in the mesh assiduously eating away the sweat and dirt and dead epidermal cells built up on my skin. It took me several more days to overcome all my instinct and learn to trust the living cloth with the more voluntary eliminations of my body also. (Previously I had been going out back to defecate in the woods, having been unable to find anything resembling a toilet, and meeting too much confusion when I tried to approach the question to dare pursue it further, for fear of encountering a taboo.)

And this was the handiwork of a child, not thirteen years of age! She could not explain to me how she had done it in any way which made sense to me. Imagine if you had to explain how to perform a reference search to someone who had not only never seen a library, but did not understand electricity, and who perhaps knew there was such a thing as written text, but did not himself read more than the alphabet. She took me once to her classroom after hours and showed me her workstation, a large wooden tray full of grayish moss, with a double row of small jars along the back each holding liquids or powders which I could only distinguish by their differing colors. Her only tools were an assortment of syringes and eyedroppers and scoops and brushes.

I went back to my house and in the growing report I would not have a chance to send for another month I wrote, *These are a priceless people. We must have them.*

The Fourth Adjustment

All these first weeks, I made no contact with any other adult. I saw them go by occasionally, and the houses around mine were occupied, but they never spoke to me or even looked at me directly. None of them objected to my squatting, but that was less implicit endorsement and more an unwillingness even to acknowledge my existence. I talked to Kitia and the other children, and tried to be patient. I hoped an opportunity would offer itself eventually for me to be of some visible use.

In the event, it was rather my lack of use which led to the break in the wall. A commotion arose in the early morning, while Kitia was showing me the plan of her wings, which she was at that age beginning to design. She would grow the parasite over the subsequent year, and was presently practicing with miniature versions, which rose from her worktable surface gossamer-thin and fluttering with an involuntary muscle-twitching. I was trying to conceal my revulsion.

Kitia looked up when the noise erupted. She casually tossed her example out of the window, to be pounced upon with a hasty scramble by several nearby birds, and went out the door. I followed her to the square: the children were gathered at the fringes, silent for once and watching. There were five women laid out on the ground, all bloody, one dead. Two of the others looked mortally wounded. They were all winged.

There were several working already on the injured, packing small brownish-white spongy masses into the open wounds and sewing them up. I would have liked to be of use, less from natural instinct than from the colder thought, which inflicted itself upon my mind, that any crisis opens social barriers. I am sorry to say I did not refrain from any noble self-censorship, but from the practical conviction that it was at once apparent my limited field-medical training could not in any valuable way be applied to the present circumstances.

I drew away, rather, to avoid being in the way as I could not turn the situation to my advantage, and in doing so ran up against Badea, who stood at the very edge of the square, observing.

She stood alone; there were no other adults nearby, and there was blood on her hands. "Are you hurt also?" I asked her.

"No," she returned, shortly.

I ventured on concern for her friends, and asked her if they had been hurt in fighting. "We have heard rumors," I added, "that the Esperigans have been encroaching on your territory." It was the first opportunity I had been given of hinting at even this much of our official sympathy, as the children only shrugged when I asked them if there were fighting going on.

She shrugged, too, with one shoulder, and the folded wing rose and fell with it. But then she said, "They leave their weapons in the forest for us, even where they cannot have gone."

The Esperigans had several kinds of land-mine technologies, including a clever mobile one which could be programmed with a target either as specific as an individual's genetic record or as general as a broadly defined body type—humanoid and winged, for instance—and set loose to wander until it found a match, then do the maximum damage it could. Only one side could carry explosive, as the other was devoted to the electronics. "The shrapnel, does it come only in one direction?" I asked, and made a fanned-out shape with my hands to illustrate. Badea looked at me sharply and nodded.

I explained the mine to her, and described their manufacture. "Some scanning devices can detect them," I added, meaning to continue into an offer, but I had not finished the litany of materials before she was striding away from the square, without another word.

I was not dissatisfied with the reaction, in which I correctly read intention to put my information to immediate use, and two days later my patience was rewarded. Badea came to my house in the mid-morning and said, "We have found one of them. Can you show us how to disarm them?"

"I am not sure," I told her, honestly. "The safest option would be to trigger it deliberately, from afar."

"The plastics they use poison the ground."

"Can you take me to its location?" I asked. She considered the question with enough seriousness that I realized there was either taboo or danger involved.

"Yes," she said finally, and took me with her to a house near the center of the village. It had steps up to the roof, and from there we could climb to that of the neighboring house, and so on until we were high enough to reach a large basket, woven not of ropes but of a kind of vine, sitting in a crook of a tree. We climbed into this, and she kicked us off from the tree.

The movement was not smooth. The nearest I can describe is the sensation of being on a child's swing, except at that highest point of weightlessness you do not go backwards, but instead go falling into another arc, but at tremendous speed, and with a pungent smell like rotten pineapple all around from the shattering of the leaves of the trees through which we were propelled. I was violently sick after some five minutes. To the comfort of my pride if not my stomach, Badea was also sick, though more efficiently and over the side, before our journey ended.

There were two other women waiting for us in the tree where we came to rest, both of them also winged: Renata and Paudi. "It's gone another three hundred meters, towards Ighlan," Renata told us—another nearby Melidan village, as they explained to me.

"If it comes near enough to pick up traces of organized habitation, it will not trigger until it is inside the settlement, among as many people as possible," I said. "It may also have a burrowing mode, if it is the more expensive kind."

They took me down through the canopy, carefully, and walked before and behind me when we came to the ground. Their wings were spread wide enough to brush against the hanging vines to either side, and they regularly leapt aloft for a brief survey. Several times they moved me with friendly hands into a slightly different path, although my untrained eyes could make no difference among the choices.

A narrow trail of large ants—the reader will forgive me for calling them ants, they were nearly indistinguishable from those efficient creatures— paced us over the forest floor, which I did not recognize as significant until we came near the mine, and I saw it covered with the ants, who did not impede its movement but milled around and over it with intense interest.

"We have adjusted them so they smell the plastic," Badea said, when I asked. "We can make them eat it," she added, "but we worried it would set off the device."

The word *adjusted* scratches at the back of my mind again as I write this, that unpleasant tinny sensation of a term that does not allow of real translation and which has been inadequately replaced. I cannot improve upon the work of the official Confederacy translators, however; to encompass the true concept would require three dry, dusty chapters more suited to a textbook on the subject of biological engineering, which I am ill-qualified to produce. I do hope that I have successfully captured the wholly casual way she spoke of this feat. Our own scientists might replicate this act of genetic sculpting in any of two dozen excellent laboratories across the Confederacy—given several years, and a suitably impressive grant. They had done it in less than two days, as a matter of course.

I did not at the time indulge in admiration. The mine was ignoring the inquisitive ants and scuttling along at a good pace, the head with its glassy eye occasionally rotating upon its spindly spider-legs, and we had half a day in which to divert it from the village ahead.

Renata followed the mine as it continued on, while I sketched what I knew of the internals in the dirt for Badea and Paudi. Any sensible mine-maker will design the device to simply explode at any interference with its working other than the disable code, so our options were not particularly satisfying. "The most likely choice," I suggested, "would be the transmitter. If it becomes unable to receive the disable code, there may be a failsafe which would deactivate it on a subsequent malfunction."

Paudi had on her back a case which, unfolded, looked very like a more elegant and compact version of little Kitia's worktable. She sat crosslegged with it on her lap and worked on it for some two hours' time, occasionally reaching down to pick up a handful of ants, which dropped into the green matrix of her table mostly curled up and died, save for a few survivors, which she herded carefully into an empty jar before taking up another sample.

I sat on the forest floor beside her, or walked with Badea, who was pacing a small circle out around us, watchfully. Occasionally she would unsling her scythe-blade, and then put it away again, and once she brought down a mottie, a small lemur-like creature. I say lemur because there is nothing closer in my experience, but it had none of the charm of an Earth-native mammal; I rather felt an instinctive disgust looking at it, even before she showed me the tiny sucker-mouths full of hooked teeth with which it latched upon a victim.

She had grown a little more loquacious, and asked me about my own homeworld. I told her about Terce, and about the seclusion of women, which she found extremely funny, as we can only laugh at the follies of those far from us which threaten us not at all. The Melidans by design maintain a five-to-one ratio of women to men, as adequate to maintain a healthy gene pool while minimizing the overall resource consumption of their population. "They cannot take the wings, so it is more difficult for them to travel," she added, with one sentence dismissing the lingering mystery which had perplexed earlier visitors, of the relative rarity of seeing their men.

She had two children, which she described to me proudly, living presently with their father and half-siblings in a village half a day's travel away, and she was considering a third. She had trained as a forest ranger, another inadequately translated term which was at the time beginning to take on a military significance among them under the pressure of the Esperigan incursions.

"I'm done," Paudi said, and we went to catch up Renata and find a nearby ant-nest, which looked like a mound of white cotton batting, rising several inches off the forest floor. Paudi introduced her small group of infected survivors into this colony, and after a little confusion and milling about, they accepted their transplantation and marched inside. The flow of departures slowed a little momentarily, then resumed, and a file split off from the main channel of workers to march in the direction of the mine.

These joined the lingering crowd still upon the mine, but the new arrivals did not stop at inspection and promptly began to struggle to insinuate themselves into the casing. We withdrew to a safe distance, watching. The mine continued on without any slackening in its pace for ten minutes, as more ants began to squeeze themselves inside, and then it hesitated, one spindly metal leg held aloft uncertainly. It went a few more slightly drunken paces, and then abruptly the legs all retracted and left it a smooth round lump on the forest floor.

The Fifth Adjustment

They showed me how to use their communications technology and grew me an interface to my own small handheld, so my report was at last able to go. Kostas began angry, of course, having been forced to defend the manner of my departure to the Esperigans without the benefit of any understanding of the circumstances, but I sent the report an hour before I messaged, and by the time we spoke he had read enough to be in reluctant agreement with my conclusions if not my methods.

I was of course full of self-satisfaction. Freed at long last from the academy and the walled gardens of Terce, armed with false confidence in my research and my training, I had so far achieved all that my design had stretched to encompass. The Esperigan blood had washed easily from my hands, and though I answered Kostas meekly when he upbraided me, privately I felt only impatience, and even he did not linger long on the topic: I had been too successful, and he had more important news.

The Esperigans had launched a small army two days before, under the more pleasant-sounding name of expeditionary defensive force. Their purpose was to establish a permanent settlement on the Melidan shore, some nine hundred miles from my present location, and begin the standard process of terraforming. The native life would be eradicated in spheres of a hundred miles across at a time: first the broad strokes of clear-cutting and the electrified nets, then the irradiation of the soil and the air, and after that the seeding of Earth-native microbes and plants. So had a thousand worlds been made over anew, and though the Esperigans had fully conquered their own continent five centuries before, they still knew the way.

He asked doubtfully if I thought some immediate resistance could be offered. Disabling a few mines scattered into the jungle seemed to him a small task. Confronting a large and organized military force was on a different order of magnitude. "I think we can do something," I said, maintaining a veneer of caution for his benefit, and took the catalog of equipment to Badea as soon as we had disengaged.

She was occupied in organizing the retrieval of the deactivated mines, which the ants were now leaving scattered in the forests and jungles. A bird-of-paradise variant had been *adjusted* to make a meal out of the ants and take the glittery mines back to their tree-top nests, where an observer might easily see them from above. She and the other collectors had so far found nearly a thousand of them. The mines made a neat pyramid, as of the harvested skulls of small cyclopean creatures with their dull eyes staring out lifelessly.

The Esperigans needed a week to cross the ocean in their numbers, and I spent it with the Melidans, developing our response. There was a heady delight in this collaboration. The work was easy and pleasant in their wide-open laboratories full of plants, roofed only with the

76

fluttering sailcloth eating sunlight to give us energy, and the best of them coming from many miles distant to participate in the effort. The Confederacy spy-satellites had gone into orbit perhaps a year after our first contact: I likely knew more about the actual force than the senior administrators of Melida. I was in much demand, consulted not only for my information but my opinion.

In the ferment of our labors, I withheld nothing. This was not yet deliberate, but neither was it innocent. I had been sent to further a war, and if in the political calculus which had arrived at this solution the lives of soldiers were only variables, yet there was still a balance I was expected to preserve. It was not my duty to give the Melidans an easy victory, any more than it had been Kostas's to give one to the Esperigans.

A short and victorious war, opening a new and tantalizing frontier for restless spirits, would at once drive up that inconvenient nationalism which is the Confederacy's worst obstacle, and render less compelling the temptations we could offer to lure them into fully joining galactic society. On the other hand, to descend into squalor, a more equal kind of civil war has often proven extremely useful, and the more lingering and bitter the better. I was sent to the Melidans in hope that, given some guidance and what material assistance we could quietly provide without taking any official position, they might be an adequate opponent for the Esperigans to produce this situation.

There has been some criticism of the officials who selected me for this mission, but in their defense, it must be pointed out it was not in fact my assignment to actually provide military assistance, nor could anyone, even myself, have envisioned my proving remotely useful in such a role. I was only meant to be an early scout. My duty was to acquire cultural information enough to open a door for a party of military experts from Voca Libre, who would not reach Melida for another two years. Ambition and opportunity promoted me, and no official hand.

I think these experts arrived sometime during the third Esperigan offensive. I cannot pinpoint the date with any accuracy, I had by then ceased to track the days, and I never met them. I hope they can forgive my theft of their war; I paid for my greed.

The Esperigans used a typical carbonized steel in most of their equipment, as bolts and hexagonal nuts and screws with star-shaped heads, and woven into the tough mesh of their body armor. This was the target of our efforts. It was a new field of endeavor for the Melidans, who used metal as they used meat, sparingly and with a sense of righteousness in

77

its avoidance. To them it was either a trace element needed in minute amounts, or an undesirable by-product of the more complicated biological processes they occasionally needed to invoke.

However, they had developed some strains of bacteria to deal with this latter waste, and the speed with which they could manipulate these organisms was extraordinary. Another quantity of the ants—a convenient delivery mechanism used by the Melidans routinely, as I learned—were adjusted to render them deficient in iron and to provide a home in their bellies for the bacteria, transforming them into shockingly efficient engines of destruction. Set loose upon several of the mines as a trial, they devoured the carapaces and left behind only smudgy black heaps of carbon dust, carefully harvested for fertilizer, and the plastic explosives from within, nestled in their bed of copper wire and silicon.

The Esperigans landed, and at once carved themselves out a neat half-moon of wasteland from the virgin shore, leaving no branches which might stretch above their encampment to offer a platform for attack. They established an electrified fence around the perimeter, with guns and patrols, and all this I observed with Badea, from a small platform in a vine-choked tree not far away: we wore the green-gray cloaks, and our faces were stained with leaf juice.

I had very little justification for inserting myself into such a role but the flimsy excuse of pointing out to Badea the most crucial section of their camp, when we had broken in. I cannot entirely say why I wished to go along on so dangerous an expedition. I am not particularly courageous. Several of my more unkind biographers have accused me of bloodlust, and pointed to this as a sequel to the disaster of my first departure. I cannot refute the accusation on the evidence, however I will point out that I chose that portion of the expedition which we hoped would encounter no violence.

But it is true I had learned already to seethe at the violent piggish blindness of the Esperigans, who would have wrecked all the wonders around me only to propagate yet another bland copy of Earth and suck dry the carcass of their own world. They were my enemy both by duty and by inclination, and I permitted myself the convenience of hating them. At the time, it made matters easier.

The wind was running from the east, and several of the Melidans attacked the camp from that side. The mines had yielded a quantity of explosive large enough to pierce the Esperigans' fence and shake the trees even as far as our lofty perch. The wind carried the smoke and dust and flames towards us, obscuring the ground and rendering the soldiers in their own camp only vague ghostlike suggestions of human shape. The fighting was hand-to-hand, and the stutter of gunfire came only tentatively through the chaos of the smoke.

Badea had been holding a narrow cord, one end weighted with a heavy seed-pod. She now poured a measure of water onto the pod, from her canteen, then flung it out into the air. It sailed over the fence and landed inside the encampment, behind one of the neat rows of storage tents. The seed pod struck the ground and immediately burst like a ripe fruit, an anemone tangle of waving roots creeping out over the ground and anchoring the cord, which she had secured at this end around one thick branch.

We let ourselves down it, hand over hand. There was none of that typical abrasion or friction which I might have expected from rope; my hands felt as cool and comfortable when we descended as when we began. We ran into the narrow space between the tents. I was experiencing that strange elongation of time which crisis can occasionally produce: I was conscious of each footfall, and of the seeming-long moments it took to place each one.

There were wary soldiers at many of the tent entrances, likely those which held either the more valuable munitions or the more valuable men. Their discipline had not faltered, even while the majority of the force was already orchestrating a response to the Melidan assault on the other side of the encampment. But we did not need to penetrate into the tents. The guards were rather useful markers for us, showing me which of the tents were the more significant. I pointed out to Badea the cluster of four tents, each guarded at either side by a pair, near the farthest end of the encampment.

Badea looked here and there over the ground as we darted under cover of smoke from one alleyway to another, the walls of waxed canvas muffling the distant shouts and the sound of gunfire. The dirt still had the yellowish tinge of Melidan soil—the Esperigans had not yet irradiated it—but it was crumbly and dry, the fine fragile native moss crushed and much torn by heavy boots and equipment, and the wind raised little dervishes of dust around our ankles.

"This ground will take years to recover fully," she said to me, soft and bitterly, as she stopped us and knelt, behind a deserted tent not far from our target. She gave me a small ceramic implement which looked much like the hair-picks sometimes worn on Terce by women with hair which never knew a blade's edge: a raised comb with three teeth, though on the tool these were much longer and sharpened at the end. I picked the ground vigorously, stabbing deep to aerate the wounded soil, while she judiciously poured out a mixture of water and certain organic extracts, and sowed a packet of seeds.

This may sound a complicated operation to be carrying out in an enemy camp, in the midst of battle, but we had practiced the maneuver, and indeed had we been glimpsed, anyone would have been hard-pressed to recognize a threat in the two gray-wrapped lumps crouched low as we pawed at the dirt. Twice while we worked, wounded soldiers were carried in a rush past either end of our alleyway, towards shelter. We were not seen.

The seeds she carried, though tiny, burst readily, and began to thrust out spiderweb-fine rootlets at such a speed they looked like nothing more than squirming maggots. Badea without concern moved her hands around them, encouraging them into the ground. When they were established, she motioned me to stop my work, and she took out the prepared ants: a much greater number of them, with a dozen of the fat yellow wasp-sized brood-mothers. Tipped out into the prepared and welcoming soil, they immediately began to burrow their way down, with the anxious harrying of their subjects and spawn.

Badea watched for a long while, crouched over, even after the ants had vanished nearly all beneath the surface. The few who emerged and darted back inside, the faint trembling of the rootlets, the shifting grains of dirt, all carried information to her. At length satisfied, she straightened saying, "Now—"

The young soldier was I think only looking for somewhere to piss, rather than investigating some noise. He came around the corner already fumbling at his belt, and seeing us did not immediately shout, likely from plain surprise, but grabbed for Badea's shoulder first. He was clean-shaven, and the name on his lapel badge was *Ridang*. I drove the soil-pick into his eye. I was taller, so the stroke went downwards, and he fell backwards to his knees away from me, clutching at his face.

He did not die at once. There must be very few deaths which come immediately, though we often like to comfort ourselves by the pretense that this failure of the body, or that injury, must at once eradicate consciousness and life and pain all together. Here sentience lasted several moments which seemed to me long: his other eye was open, and looked at me while his hands clawed for the handle of the pick. When this had faded, and he had fallen supine to the ground, there was yet a convulsive movement of all the limbs and a trickling of blood from mouth and nose and eye before the final stiffening jerk left the body emptied and inanimate.

I watched him die in a strange parody of serenity, all feeling hollowed out of me, and then turning away vomited upon the ground. Behind me, Badea cut open his belly and his thighs and turned him face down onto the dirt, so the blood and the effluvia leaked out of him. "That will do a little good for the ground at least, before they carry him away to waste him," she said. "Come." She touched my shoulder, not unkindly, but I flinched from the touch as from a blow.

It was not that Badea or her fellows were indifferent to death, or casual towards murder. But there is a price to be paid for living in a world whose native hostilities have been cherished rather than crushed. Melidan life expectancy is some ten years beneath that of Confederacy citizens, though they are on average healthier and more fit both genetically and physically. In their philosophy a human life is not inherently superior and to be valued over any other kind. Accident and predation claim many, and living intimately with the daily cruelties of nature dulls the facility for sentiment. Badea enjoyed none of that comforting distance which allows us to think ourselves assured of the full potential span of life, and therefore suffered none of the pangs when confronted with evidence to the contrary. I looked at my victim and saw my own face; so too did she, but she had lived all her life so aware, and it did not bow her shoulders.

Five days passed before the Esperigan equipment began to come apart. Another day halted all their work, and in confusion they retreated to their encampment. I did not go with the Melidan company that destroyed them to the last man.

Contrary to many accusations, I did not lie to Kostas in my report and pretend surprise. I freely confessed to him I had expected the result, and truthfully explained I had not wished to make claims of which I was unsure. I never deliberately sought to deceive any of my superiors or conceal information from them, save in such small ways. At first I was not Melidan enough to wish to do so, and later I was too Melidan to feel anything but revulsion at the concept.

He and I discussed our next steps in the tiger-dance. I described as best I could the Melidan technology, and after consultation with various Confederacy experts, it was agreed he would quietly mention to the Esperigan minister of defense, at their weekly luncheon, a particular Confederacy technology: ceramic coatings, which could be ordered at vast expense and two years' delay from Bel Rios. Or, he would suggest, if the Esperigans wished to deed some land to the Confederacy, a private entrepreneurial concern might fund the construction of a local fabrication plant, and produce them at much less cost, in six months' time.

The Esperigans took the bait, and saw only private greed behind this apparent breach of neutrality: imagining Kostas an investor in this private concern, they winked at his veniality, and eagerly helped us to their own exploitation. Meanwhile, they continued occasional and tentative incursions into the Melidan continent, probing the coastline, but the disruption they created betrayed their attempts, and whichever settlement was nearest would at once deliver them a present of the industrious ants, so these met with no greater success than the first.

Through these months of brief and grudging detente, I traveled extensively throughout the continent. My journals are widely available, being the domain of our government, but they are shamefully sparse, and I apologize to my colleagues for it. I would have been more diligent in my work if I had imagined I would be the last and not the first such chronicler. At the time, giddy with success, I went with more the spirit of a holidaymaker than a researcher, and I sent only those images and notes which it was pleasant to me to record, with the excuse of limited capacity to send my reports.

For what cold comfort it may be, I must tell you photography and description are inadequate to convey the experience of standing in the living heart of a world, alien yet not hostile, and when I walked hand in hand with Badea along the crest of a great canyon wall and looked down over the ridges of purple and grey and ochre at the gently waving tendrils of an elacca forest, which in my notorious video recordings can provoke nausea in nearly every observer, I felt the first real stir of an unfamiliar sensation of beauty-in-strangeness, and I laughed in delight and surprise, while she looked at me and smiled.

We returned to her village three days later and saw the bombing as we came, the new Esperigan long-range fighter planes like narrow silver knife-blades making low passes overhead, the smoke rising black and oily against the sky. Our basket-journey could not be accelerated, so we could only cling to the sides and wait as we were carried onward. The planes and the smoke were gone before we arrived; the wreckage was not.

I was angry at Kostas afterwards, unfairly. He was no more truly the Esperigans' confidant than they were his, but I felt at the time that it was his business to know what they were about, and he had failed to warn me. I accused him of deliberate concealment; he told me, censoriously, that I had known the risk when I had gone to the continent, and he could hardly be responsible for preserving my safety while I slept in the very war zone. This silenced my tirade, as I realized how near I had come to betraying myself. Of course he would not have wanted me to warn the Melidans; it had not yet occurred to him I would have wished to, myself. I ought not have wanted to.

Forty-three people were killed in the attack. Kitia was yet lingering when I came to her small bedside. She was in no pain, her eyes cloudy and distant, already withdrawing; her family had been and gone again. "I knew you were coming back, so I asked them to let me stay a little longer," she told me. "I wanted to say goodbye." She paused and added uncertainly, "And I was afraid, a little. Don't tell."

I promised her I would not. She sighed and said, "I shouldn't wait any longer. Will you call them over?"

The attendant came when I raised my hand, and he asked Kitia, "Are you ready?"

"Yes," she said, a little doubtful. "It won't hurt?"

"No, not at all," he said, already taking out with a gloved hand a small flat strip from a pouch, filmy green and smelling of raspberries. Kitia opened her mouth, and he laid it on her tongue. It dissolved almost at once, and she blinked twice and was asleep. Her hand went cold a few minutes later, still lying between my own.

I stood with her family when we laid her to rest, the next morning. The attendants put her carefully down in a clearing, and sprayed her from a distance, the smell of cut roses just going to rot, and stepped back. Her parents wept noisily; I stayed dry-eyed as any seemly Terce matron, displaying my assurance of the ascension of the dead. The birds came first, and the motties, to pluck at her eyes and her lips, and the beetles hurrying with a hum of eager jaws to deconstruct her into raw parts. They did not have long to feast: the forest itself was devouring her from below in a green tide rising, climbing in small creepers up her cheeks and displacing them all.

When she was covered over, the mourners turned away and went to join the shared wake behind us in the village square. They threw uncertain and puzzled looks at my remaining as they went past, and at my tearless face. But she was not yet gone: there was a suggestion of a girl lingering there, a collapsing scaffold draped in an unhurried carpet of living things. I did not leave, though behind me there rose a murmur of noise as the families of the dead spoke reminiscences of their lost ones.

Near dawn, the green carpeting slipped briefly. In the dim watery light I glimpsed for one moment an emptied socket full of beetles, and I wept.

The Sixth Adjustment

I will not claim, after this, that I took the wings only from duty, but I refute the accusation I took them in treason. There was no other choice. Men and children and the elderly or the sick, all the wingless, were fleeing from the continuing hail of Esperigan attacks. They were retreating deep into the heart of the continent, beyond the refueling range for the Esperigan warcraft, to shelters hidden so far in caves and in overgrowth that even my spy satellites knew nothing of them. My connection to Kostas would have been severed, and if I could provide neither intelligence nor direct assistance, I might as well have slunk back to the embassy, and saved myself the discomfort of being a refugee. Neither alternative was palatable.

They laid me upon the altar like a sacrifice, or so I felt, though they gave me something to drink which calmed my body, the nervous and involuntary twitching of my limbs and skin. Badea sat at my head and held the heavy long braid of my hair out of the way, while the others depilated my back and wiped it with alcohol. They bound me down then, and slit my skin open in two lines mostly parallel to the spine. Then Paudi gently set the wings upon me.

I lacked the skill to grow my own, in the time we had; Badea and Paudi helped me to mine so that I might stay. But even with the little assistance I had been able to contribute, I had seen more than I wished to of the parasites, and despite my closed eyes, my face turned downwards, I knew to my horror that the faint curious feather-brush sensation was the intrusion of the fine spiderweb filaments, each fifteen feet long, which now wriggled into the hospitable environment of my exposed inner flesh and began to sew themselves into me.

Pain came and went as the filaments worked their way through muscle and bone, finding one bundle of nerves and then another. After the first half hour, Badea told me gently, "It's coming to the spine," and gave me another drink. The drug kept my body from movement, but could do nothing to numb the agony. I cannot describe it adequately. If you have ever managed to inflict food poisoning upon yourself, despite all the Confederacy's safeguards, you may conceive of the kind if not the degree of suffering, an experience which envelops the whole body, every muscle and joint, and alters not only your physical self but your thoughts: all vanishes but pain, and the question, is the worst over? which is answered *no* and *no* again.

But at some point the pain began indeed to ebb. The filaments had entered the brain, and it is a measure of the experience that what I had feared the most was now blessed relief; I lay inert and closed my eyes gratefully while sensation spread outward from my back, and my new-borrowed limbs became gradually indeed my own, flinching from the currents of the air, and the touch of my friends' hands upon me. Eventually I slept.

The Seventh Adjustment

The details of the war, which unfolded now in earnest, I do not need to recount again. Kostas kept excellent records, better by far than my own, and students enough have memorized the dates and geographic coordinates, bounding death and ruin in small numbers. Instead I will tell you that from aloft, the Esperigans' poisoned-ground encampments made half-starbursts of ochre brown and withered yellow, outlines like tentacles crawling into the healthy growth around them. Their supply-ships anchored out to sea glazed the water with a slick of oil and refuse, while the soldiers practiced their shooting on the vast schools of slow-swimming kraken young, whose bloated white bodies floated to the surface and drifted away along the coast, so many they defied even the appetite of the sharks.

I will tell you that when we painted their hulls with algaes and small crustacean-like borers, our work was camouflaged by great blooms of sea day-lilies around the ships, their masses throwing up reflected red color on the steel to hide the quietly creeping rust until the first winter storms struck and the grown kraken came to the surface to feed. I will tell you we watched from shore while the ships broke and foundered, and the teeth of the kraken shone like fire opals in the explosions, and if we wept, we wept only for the soiled ocean.

Still more ships came, and more planes; the ceramic coatings arrived, and more soldiers with protected guns and bombs and sprayed poisons, to fend off the altered motties and the little hybrid sparrowlike birds, their sharp cognizant eyes chemically retrained to see the Esperigan uniform colors as enemy markings. We planted acids and more aggressive species of plants along their supply lines, so their communications remained hopeful rather than reliable, and ambushed them at night; they carved into the forest with axes and power-saws and vast strip-miners, which ground to a halt and fell to pieces, choking on vines which hardened to the tensile strength of steel as they matured.

Contrary to claims which were raised at my trial *in absentia* and disproven with communication logs, throughout this time I spoke to Kostas regularly. I confused him, I think; I gave him all the intelligence which he needed to convey to the Esperigans, that they might respond to the next Melidan foray, but I did not conceal my feelings or the increasing complication of my loyalties, objecting to him bitterly and with personal anger about Esperigan attacks. I misled him with honesty: he thought, I believe, that I was only spilling a natural frustration to him, and through that airing clearing out my own doubts. But I had only lost the art of lying.

There is a general increase of perception which comes with the wings, the nerves teased to a higher pitch of awareness. All the little fidgets and twitches of lying betray themselves more readily, so only the more twisted forms can evade detection—where the speaker first deceives herself, or the wholly casual deceit of the sociopath who feels no remorse. This was the root of the Melidan disgust of the act, and I had acquired it.

If Kostas had known, he would at once have removed me: a diplomat is not much use if she cannot lie at need, much less an agent. But I did not volunteer the information, and indeed I did not realize, at first, how fully I had absorbed the stricture. I did not realize at all, until Badea came to me, three years into the war. I was sitting alone and in the dark by the communications console, the phosphorescent after-image of Kostas's face fading into the surface.

She sat down beside me and said, "The Esperigans answer us too quickly. Their technology advances in these great leaps, and every time we press them back, they return in less than a month to very nearly the same position."

I thought, at first, that this was the moment: that she meant to ask me about membership in the Confederacy. I felt no sense of satisfaction, only a weary kind of resignation. The war would end, the Esperigans would follow, and in a few generations they would both be eaten up by bureaucracy and standards and immigration.

Instead Badea looked at me and said, "Are your people helping them, also?"

My denial ought to have come without thought, leapt easily off the tongue with all the conviction duty could give it, and been followed by invitation. Instead I said nothing, my throat closed involuntarily. We sat silently in the darkness, and at last she said, "Will you tell me why?"

I felt at the time I could do no more harm, and perhaps some good, by honesty. I told her all the rationale, and expressed all our willingness to receive them into our union as equals. I went so far as to offer her the platitudes with which we convince ourselves we are justified in our slow gentle imperialism: that unification is necessary and advances all together, bringing peace.

She only shook her head and looked away from me. After a moment, she said, "Your people will never stop. Whatever we devise, they will help the Esperigans to a counter, and if the Esperigans devise some weapon we cannot defend ourselves against, they will help us, and we will batter each other into limp exhaustion, until in the end we all fall."

86

"Yes," I said, because it was true. I am not sure I was still able to lie, but in any case I did not know, and I did not lie.

I was not permitted to communicate with Kostas again until they were ready. Thirty-six of the Melidans' greatest designers and scientists died in the effort. I learned of their deaths in bits and pieces. They worked in isolated and quarantined spaces, their every action recorded even as the viruses and bacteria they were developing killed them. It was a little more than three months before Badea came to me again.

We had not spoken since the night she had learned the duplicity of the Confederacy's support and my own. I could not ask her forgiveness, and she could not give it. She did not come for reconciliation but to send a message to the Esperigans and to the Confederacy through me.

I did not comprehend at first. But when I did, I knew enough to be sure she was neither lying nor mistaken, and to be sure the threat was very real. The same was not true of Kostas, and still less of the Esperigans. My frantic attempts to persuade them worked instead to the contrary end. The long gap since my last communique made Kostas suspicious: he thought me a convert, or generously a manipulated tool.

"If they had the capability, they would have used it already," he said, and if I could not convince him, the Esperigans would never believe.

I asked Badea to make a demonstration. There was a large island broken off the southern coast of the Esperigan continent, thoroughly settled and industrialized, with two substantial port cities. Sixty miles separated it from the mainland. I proposed the Melidans should begin there, where the attack might be contained.

"No," Badea said. "So your scientists can develop a counter? No. We are done with exchanges."

The rest you know. A thousand coracles left Melidan shores the next morning, and by sundown on the third following day, the Esperigan cities were crumbling. Refugees fled the groaning skyscrapers as they slowly bowed under their own weight. The trees died; the crops also, and the cattle, all the life and vegetation that had been imported from Earth and square-peg forced into the new world stripped bare for their convenience.

Meanwhile in the crowded shelters the viruses leapt easily from one victim to another, rewriting their genetic lines. Where the changes took hold, the altered survived. The others fell to the same deadly plagues that consumed all Earth-native life. The native Melidan moss crept in a swift green carpet over the corpses, and the beetle-hordes with it.

I can give you no first-hand account of those days. I too lay fevered and sick while the alteration ran its course in me, though I was tended better, and with more care, by my sisters. When I was strong enough to rise, the waves of death were over. My wings curled limply over my shoulders as I walked through the empty streets of Landfall, pavement stones pierced and broken by hungry vines, like bones cracked open for marrow. The moss covered the dead, who filled the shattered streets.

The squat embassy building had mostly crumpled down on one corner, smashed windows gaping hollow and black. A large pavilion of simple cotton fabric had been raised in the courtyard, to serve as both hospital and headquarters. A young undersecretary of state was the senior diplomat remaining. Kostas had died early, he told me. Others were still in the process of dying, their bodies waging an internal war that left them twisted by hideous deformities.

Less than one in thirty, was his estimate of the survivors. Imagine yourself on an air-train in a crush, and then imagine yourself suddenly alone but for one other passenger across the room, a stranger staring at you. Badea called it a sustainable population.

The Melidans cleared the spaceport of vegetation, though little now was left but the black-scorched landing pad, Confederacy manufacture, all of woven carbon and titanium.

"Those who wish may leave," Badea said. "We will help the rest."

Most of the survivors chose to remain. They looked at their faces in the mirror, flecked with green, and feared the Melidans less than their welcome on another world.

I left by the first small ship that dared come down to take off refugees, with no attention to the destination or the duration of the voyage. I wished only to be away. The wings were easily removed. A quick and painful amputation of the gossamer and fretwork which protruded from the flesh, and the rest might be left for the body to absorb slowly. The strange muffled quality of the world, the sensation of numbness, passed eventually. The two scars upon my back, parallel lines, I will keep the rest of my days.

Afterword

I spoke with Badea once more before I left. She came to ask me why I was going, to what end I thought I went. She would be perplexed, I think, to see me in my little cottage here on Reivaldt, some hundred miles from the nearest city, although she would have liked the small flowerlike lieden which live on the rocks of my garden wall, one of the few remnants of the lost native fauna which have survived the terraforming outside the preserves of the university system.

I left because I could not remain. Every step I took on Melida, I felt dead bones cracking beneath my feet. The Melidans did not kill lightly, an individual or an ecosystem, nor any more effectually than do we. If the Melidans had not let the plague loose upon the Esperigans, we would have destroyed them soon enough ourselves, and the Melidans with them. But we distance ourselves better from our murders, and so are not prepared to confront them. My wings whispered to me gently when I passed Melidans in the green-swathed cemetary streets, that they were not sickened, were not miserable. There was sorrow and regret but no self-loathing, where I had nothing else. I was alone.

When I came off my small vessel here, I came fully expecting punishment, even longing for it, a judgment which would at least be an end. Blame had wandered through the halls of state like an unwanted child, but when I proved willing to adopt whatever share anyone cared to mete out to me, to confess any crime which was convenient and to proffer no defense, it turned contrary, and fled.

Time enough has passed that I can be grateful now to the politicians who spared my life and gave me what passes for my freedom. In the moment, I could scarcely feel enough even to be happy that my report contributed some little to the abandonment of any reprisal against Melida: as though we ought hold them responsible for defying our expectations not of their willingness to kill one another, but only of the extent of their ability.

But time does not heal all wounds. I am often asked by visitors whether I would ever return to Melida. I will not. I am done with politics and the great concerns of the universe of human settlement. I am content to sit in my small garden, and watch the ants at work.

Ruth Patrona

First published in *Warriors 2*,
edited by Gardner Dozois and George R. R. Martin, 2010.

ABOUT THE AUTHOR

Born in New York City, where she still lives with her mystery-editor husband and six computers, **Naomi Novik** is a first-generation American who was raised on Polish fairy tales, Baba Yaga, and Tolkien. After doing graduate work in Computer Science at Columbia University, she participated in the development of the computer game *Neverwinter Nights: Shadows of Undrentide,* and then decided to try her hand at novels. A good decision! The resultant Temeraire series—consisting of *Temeraire, His Majesty's Dragon, Black Powder War, The*

Throne of Jade, Tongue of Serpents, Victory of Eagles, Empire of Ivory, Crucible of Gold, and *Blood of Tyrants*—describing an alternate version of the Napoleonic Wars where dragons are used as living weapons, has been phenomenally popular and successful. Coming up is a new non-Temeraire fantasy novel, *Uprooted.*

Nevermore

IAN R. MACLEOD

Now that he couldn't afford to buy enough reality, Gustav had no option but to paint what he saw in his dreams. With no sketchpad to bring back, no palette or cursor, his head rolling up from the pillow and his mouth dry and his jaw aching from the booze he'd drunk the evening before—which was the cheapest means he'd yet found of getting to sleep—he was left with just that one chance, and few trailing wisps of something that might once have been beautiful before he had to face the void of the day.

It hadn't started like this, but he could see by now that this was how it had probably ended. Representational art had had its heydays, and for a while he'd been feted like the bright new talent he'd once been sure he was. And big lumpy actuality that you could smell and taste and get under your fingernails would probably come back into style again—long after it had ceased to matter to him.

So that was it. Load upon load of self-pity falling down upon him this morning from the damp-stained ceiling. What *had* he been dreaming? Something—surely something. Otherwise being here and being Gustav wouldn't come as this big a jolt. He should've got more used to it than this by now . . . Gustav scratched himself, and discovered that he also had an erection, which was another sign—hadn't he read once, somewhere?—that you'd been dreaming dreams of the old-fashioned kind, unsimulated, unaided. A sign, anyway, of a kind of biological optimism. The hope that there might just be a hope.

Arthritic, Cro-Magnon, he wandered out from his bed. Knobbled legs, knobbled veins, knobbled toes. He still missed the habit of fiddling with the controls of his window in the pock-marked far wall, changing the perspectives and the light in the dim hope that he might stumble across something better. The sun and the moon were blazing down over Paris from their respective quadrants, pouring like mercury through the nanosmog. He pressed his hand to the glass, feeling the watery wheeze of the crack that now snaked across it. Five stories up in these scrawny empty tenements, and a long, long way down. He laid his forehead against its coolness as the sour thought that he might try to paint this scene speeded through him. He'd finished at least twenty paintings of foreal Paris; all reality engines and cabled ruins in grey, black, and white. Probably done, oh, at least several hundred studies in ink-wash, pencil, charcoal. No one would ever buy them, and for once they were right. The things were passionless, ugly—he pitied the potentially lovely canvases he'd ruined to make them. He pulled back from the window and looked down at himself. His erection had faded from sight beneath his belly.

Gustav shuffled through food wrappers and scrunched-up bits of cartridge paper. Leaning drifts of canvas frames turned their backs from him towards the walls, whispering on breaths of turpentine of things that might once have been. But that was okay because he didn't have any paint right now. Maybe later, he'd get the daft feeling that, today, something might work out, and he'd sell himself for a few credits in some stupid trick or other—what had it been last time; painting roses red dressed as a playing card?—and the supply ducts would bear him a few precious tubes of oils. And a few hours after that he'd be—but what that noise?

A thin white droning like a plastic insect. In fact, it had been there all along—had probably woken him at this ridiculous hour—but had seemed so much a part of everything else that he hadn't noticed. Gustav looked around, tilting his head until his better ear located the source. He slid a sticky avalanche of canvas board and cotton paper off an old chair, and burrowed in the cushions until his hand closed on a telephone. He'd only kept the thing because it was so cheap that the phone company hadn't bothered to disconnect the line when he'd stopped paying. That was, if the telephone company still existed. It was chipped from the time he'd thrown it across the room after his last conversation with his agent. But he touched the activate pad anyway, not expecting anything more than a blip in the system, white machine noise.

"Gustav, you're still *there* are you?"

He stared at the mouthpiece. It was his dead ex-wife Elanore's voice.

"What do you want?"

"Don't be like that, Gus. Well, *I* won't be anyway. Time's passed, you know, things have changed."

"Sure, and you're going to tell me next that you—"

"—Yes, would like to meet up. We're arranging this party. I ran into Marcel in Venice—he's currently Doge there, you know—and we got talking about old times and all the old gang. And so we decided we were due for a reunion. You've been one of the hardest ones to find, Gus. And then I remembered that old tenement . . . "

"Like you say, I'm still here."

"Still painting?"

"Of course I'm still painting. It's what I do."

"That's great. Well—sorry to give you so little time, but the whole thing's fixed for this evening. You won't believe what everyone's up to now. But then I suppose you've seen Francine across the sky."

"Look, I'm not sure that I—"

"—And we're going for Paris, 1890. Should be right up your street. I've splashed out on all-senses. And the food and the drink'll be foreal. So you'll come, won't you? The past is the past and I've honestly forgotten about much of it since I passed on. Put it into context, anyway. I really don't bear a grudge. So you will come? Remember how it was, Gus? Just smile for me the way you used to. And remember . . . "

Of course he remembered. But he still didn't know what the hell to expect that evening as he waited—too early, despite the fact that he'd done his best to be pointedly late—in the virtual glow of a pavement café off the Rue St-Jacques beneath a sky fuzzy with Van Gogh stars.

Searching the daubed figures strolling along the cobbles, Gustav spotted Elanore coming long before she saw him. He raised a hand and she came over, sitting down on a wobbly chair at the uneven swirl of the table. Doing his best to maintain a grumpy pause, Gustav called the waiter for wine and raised his glass to her with trembling fingers. He swallowed it all down. Just as she'd promised, the stuff was foreal.

Elanore smiled at him. And Elanore looked beautiful. Elanore was dressed for the era in a long dress of pure ultramarine. Her red hair was bunched up beneath a narrow-brimmed hat adorned with flowers.

"It's about now," she said, "that you tell me I haven't changed."

"And you tell me that I have."

She nodded. "But it's true. Although you haven't changed *that* much, Gus. You've aged, but you're still one of the most . . . solid people I know."

Elanore offered him a Disc Bleu. He took it although he hadn't smoked in years and she'd always complained that the things were bad for him when she was alive. Elanore's skin felt cool and dry in the moment that their hands touched, and the taste of the smoke as it shimmered amid the brush strokes was just as it had always been. Music drifted out from the blaze of the bar where dark figures writhed as if in flames. Any moment now, he knew, she'd try to say something vaguely conciliatory, and he'd interrupt as he attempted to do the same.

He gestured around at the daubs and smears of the other empty tables. He said, "I thought I was going to be late . . . " The underside of the canopy that stretched across the pavement blazed. How poor old Vincent had loved his cadmiums and chromes. And never sold one single fucking painting in his entire life.

"What—what I told you was true," Elanore said, stumbling slightly over these little words, sounding almost un-Elanore-like for a moment; nearly uneasy. "I mean, about Marcel in Venice and Francine across the sky. And, yes, we *did* talk about a reunion. But you know how these things are. Time's precious and, at the end of the day it's been so long that these things really do take a lot of nerve. So it didn't come off. It was just a few promises that no one really imagined they'd keep. But I thought—well I thought that it would be nice to see you anyway. At least one more time."

"So all of this is just for me. *Jesus*, Elanore, I knew you were rich, but . . . "

"Don't be like that, Gustav. I'm not trying to impress you or depress you or whatever. It was just the way it came out."

He poured more of the wine, wondering as he did so exactly what trick it was that allowed them to share it.

"So you're still painting?"

"Yep."

"I haven't seen much of your work about."

"I do it for private clients," Gustav said. "Mostly."

He glared at Elanore, daring her to challenge his statement. Of course, if he really was painting and selling, he'd have some credit. And if he had credit, he wouldn't be living in that dreadful tenement she'd tracked him down to. He'd have paid for all the necessary treatments to stop himself becoming the frail old man he so nearly was. *I can help, you know,* Gustav could hear Elanore saying because he'd heard her say it so many times before. *I don't need all this wealth. So let me give you just a little help. Give me that chance . . .* But what she actually said was even worse.

"Are you recording yourself, Gus?" Elanore asked. "Do you have a librarian?"

Now, he thought, now is the time to walk out. Pull this whole thing down and go back into the street—the foreal street. And forget.

"Did you know," he said instead, "that the word reality once actually meant foreal—not the projections and the simulations, but proper actuality. But then along came *virtual* reality, and of course when the next generation of products was developed the illusion was so much better that you could walk right into it instead of having to put on goggles and a suit. So they had to think of an improved phrase, a super-word for the purposes of marketing. And someone must have said, *Why don't we just call it reality?*"

"You don't have to be hurtful, Gus. There's no rule written down that says we can't get on."

"I thought that that was exactly the problem. It's in my head, and it was probably there in yours before you died. Now it's . . . " He'd have said more. But he was suddenly, stupidly, near to tears.

"What exactly *are* you doing these days, Gus?" she asked as he cleared his throat and pretended it was the wine that he'd choked on. "What are you painting at the moment?"

"I'm working on a series," he was surprised to hear himself saying. "It's a sort of a journey-piece. A sequence of paintings which begin here in Paris and then . . . " He swallowed. " . . . bright, dark colors . . . " A nerve began to leap beside his eye. Something seemed to touch him, but was too faint to be heard or felt or seen.

"Sounds good, Gus," Elanore said, leaning towards him across the table. And Elanore smelled of Elanore the way she always did. Her pale skin was freckled from the sunlight of whatever warm and virtual place she was living. Across her cheeks and her upper lip, threaded gold, lay the down that he'd brushed so many times with his the tips of his fingers. "I can tell from that look in your eyes that you're into a really good phase . . . "

After that, things went better. They shared a second bottle of *vin ordinaire.* They made a little mountain of the butts of her Disc Bleu in the ashtray. This ghost—she really was like Elanore. Gustav didn't even object to her taking his hand across the table. There was a kind of abandon in all of this—new ideas mixed with old memories. And he understood more clearly now what Van Gogh had meant about this café being a place where you could ruin oneself, or go mad or commit a crime.

The few other diners faded. The virtual waiters, their aprons a single assured grey-white stroke of the palette knife, started to tip the chairs against the tables. The aromas of the Left Bank's ever-unreliable sewers began to override those of cigarettes and people and horse dung and wine. At least, Gustav thought, *that* was still foreal . . .

"I suppose quite a lot of the others have died by now," Gustav said. "All that facile gang you seem to so fondly remember."

"People still change, you know. Just because we've passed on doesn't mean we can't change."

By now, he was in a mellow enough mood just to nod at that. And how have you changed, Elanore? he wondered. After so long, what flicker of the electrons made you decide to come to me now?

"You're obviously doing well."

"I am . . . " She nodded, as if the idea surprised her. "I mean, I didn't expect—"

"—And you look—"

"—And you, Gus, what I said about you being—"

"—That project of mine—"

"—I know, I—"

They stopped and gazed at each other. Then they both smiled and the moment seemed to hold, warm and frozen, as if from a scene within a painting. It was almost . . .

"Well . . . " Elanore broke the illusion first as she began to fumble in the small sequined purse she had on her lap. Eventually, she produced a handkerchief and blew delicately on her nose. Gustav tried not to grind his teeth—although this was exactly the kind of affectation he detested about ghosts. He guessed, anyway, from the changed look on her face, that she knew what he was thinking. "I suppose that's it, then, isn't it, Gus? We've met—we've spent the evening together without arguing. Almost like old times."

"Nothing will ever be like old times."

"No . . . " Her eyes glinted, and he thought for a moment that she was going to become angry—goaded at last into something like the Elanore of old. But she just smiled. "Nothing ever will be like old times. That's the problem, isn't it? Nothing ever was, or ever will be . . . "

Elanore clipped her purse shut again. Elanore stood up. Gustav saw her hesitate as she considered bending down to kiss him farewell, then decide that he would just regard that as another affront, another slap in the face.

Elanore turned and walked away from Gustav, fading into the chiaroscuro swirls of lamplight and grey.

Elanore, as if Gustav needed reminding, had been alive when he'd first met her. In fact, he'd never known anyone who was more so. Of course, the age difference between them was always huge—she'd already been past a hundred by then and he was barely forty—but they'd agreed on that first day that they met and on many days after that there was a corner in time around which the old eventually turned to rejoin the young.

In another age, and although she always laughingly denied it, Gustav always suspected that Elanore would have had her sagging breasts implanted with silicone, the wrinkles stretched back from her face, her heart replaced by a throbbing steel simulacrum. But she was lucky enough to exist at a time when effective anti-aging treatments were finally available. As a post-centenarian, wise and rich and moderately, pleasantly, famous, Elanore was probably more fresh and beautiful than she'd been at any other era in her life. Gustav had met her at a party beside a Russian lake—guests wandering amid dunes of snow. Foreal had been a fashionable option then; although for Gustav the grounds of this pillared ice-crystalled palace that Catherine the Great's Scottish favorite Charles Cameron had built seemed far too gorgeous to be entirely true. But it *was* true—foreal, actual, concrete, genuine, unvirtual—and such knowledge was what had driven him then. That, and the huge impossibility of ever really managing to convey any of it as a painter. That, and the absolute certainty that he would try.

Elanore had wandered up to him from the forest dusk dressed in seal furs. The shock of her beauty had been like all the rubbish he'd heard other artists talk about and thus so detested. And he'd been a stammering wreck, but somehow that hadn't mattered. There had been—and here again the words became stupid, meaningless—a dazed physicality between them from that first moment that was so intense it was spiritual.

Elanore told Gustav that she'd seen and admired the series of triptychs he'd just finished working on. They were painted directly onto slabs of wood, and depicted totemistic figures in dense blocks of color. The critics had generally dammed them with faint praise—had talked of Cubism and Mondrian—were somehow unable to recognize Gustav's obvious and grateful debt to Gauguin's Tahitian paintings. But Elanore had seen and understood those bright muddy colors. And, yes, she'd dabbled a little in painting herself—just enough to know that truly creative acts were probably beyond her . . .

Elanore wore her red hair short in those days. And there were freckles, then as always, scattered across the bridge of her nose. She showed the tips of her teeth when she smiled, and he was conscious of her lips and her tongue. He could smell, faint within the clouds of breath that entwined them, her womanly scent.

A small black cat threaded its way between them as they talked, then, barely breaking the crust of the snow, leapt up onto a bough of the nearest pine and crouched there, watching them with emerald eyes.

"That's Metzengerstein," Elanore said, her own even greener eyes flickering across Gustav face, but never ceasing to regard him. "He's my librarian."

When they made love later on in the agate pavilion's frozen glow and as the smoke of their breath and their sweat clouded the winter twilight, all the disparate elements of Gustav's world finally seemed to join. He carved Elanore's breasts with his fingers and tongue and painted her with her juices and plunged into her sweet depths and came, finally, finally, and quite deliciously, as her fingers slid around and he in turn was parted and entered by her.

Swimming back up from that, soaked with Elanore, exhausted, but his cock amazingly still half-stiff and rising, Gustav became conscious of the black cat that all this time had been threading its way between them. Its tail now curled against his thigh, corrugating his scrotum. Its claws gently kneaded his belly.

Elanore had laughed and picked Metzengerstein up, purring herself as she laid the creature between her breasts.

Gustav understood. Then or later, there was never any need for her to say more. After all, even Elanore couldn't live forever—and she needed a librarian with her to record her thoughts and actions if she was ever to pass on. For all its myriad complexities, the human brain had evolved to last a single lifetime; after that, the memories and impressions eventually began to overflow, the data became corrupted. Yes, Gustav understood. He even came to like the way Metzengerstein followed Elanore around like a witch's familiar, and, yes, its soft sharp cajolings as they made love.

Did they call them ghosts then? Gustav couldn't remember. It was a word, anyway—like spic, or nigger—that you never used in front of them. When he and Elanore were married, when Gustav loved and painted and loved and painted her, when she gave him her life and her spirit and his own career somehow began to take off as he finally mastered the trick of getting some of the passion he felt down onto the lovely, awkward canvas, he always knew that part of the intensity between them came from the age gap, the difference, the inescapable fact that Elanore would soon have to die.

It finally happened, he remembered, when he was leaving Gauguin's tropic dreams and nightmares behind and toying with a more straight-forwardly Impressionist phase. Elanore was modelling for him nude as Manet's *Olympia*. As a concession to practicalities and to the urgency that then always possessed him when he was painting, the black maid-servant bearing the flowers in his lavish new studio on the Boulevard des Capucines was a projection, but the divan and all the hangings, the flowers, and the cat, of course—although by its programmed natured Metzengerstein was incapable of looking quite as scared and scrawny as Manet's original—were all foreal.

"You know," Elanore said, not breaking pose, one hand toying with the hem of the shawl on which she was lying, the other laid negligently, possessively, without modesty, across her pubic triangle, "we really should re-invite Marcel over after all he's done for us lately."

"Marcel?" In honesty, Gustav was paying little attention to anything at that moment other than which shade to swirl into the boudoir darkness. He dabbed again onto his testing scrap. "Marcel's in San Francisco. We haven't seen him in months."

"Of course . . . Silly me."

He finally glanced up again what could have been moments or minutes later, suddenly aware that a cold silence that had set in. Elanore, being Elanore, never forgot anything. Elanore was light and life. Now, all her *Olympia*-like poise was gone.

This wasn't like the decay and loss of function that affected the elderly in the days before recombinant drugs. Just like her heart and her limbs, Elanore's physical brain still functioned perfectly. But the effect was the same. Confusions and mistakes happened frequently after that, as if consciousness drained rapidly once the initial rent was made. For Elanore, with her exquisite dignity, her continued beauty, her companies and her investments and the contacts that she needed to maintain, the process of senility was particularly terrible. No one, least of all Gustav, argued against her decision to pass on.

Back where reality ended, it was past midnight and the moon was blazing down over the Left Bank's broken rooftops through the greyish brown nanosmog. And exactly where, Gustav wondered, glaring up at it through the still humming gantries of the reality engine that had enclosed him and Elanore, is Francine across the sky? How much do you have to pay to get the right decoders in your optic nerves and see the stars entwined in some vast projection of her? How much of your life do you have to give away?

The mazy streets behind St-Michael were rotten and weed-grown in the bilious fog, the dulled moonlight. No one but Gustav seems to live in the half-supported ruins of the Left Bank nowadays. It was just a place for posing in and being seen—although in that respect, Gustav reflected, things really hadn't changed. To get back to his tenement, he had to cross the Boulevard St-Germain through a stream of buzzing robot cars that, no matter how he dodged them, still managed to avoid him. In the busier streets beyond, the big reality engines were still glowing. In fact, it was said that you could now go from one side of Paris to the other without having to step out into foreal. Gustav, as ever, did his best to do the opposite although he knew that, even without any credit, he would still be freely admitted to the many realities on offer in these generous, carefree days. He scowled at the shining planes of the powerfields that stretched between the gantries like bubbles. Faintly from inside, coming at him from beyond the humming of the transformers that tamed and organized the droplets of nanosmog into shapes you could feel, odors you could smell, chairs you could sit on, he could hear words and laughter, music, the clink of glasses. He could even just make out the shapes of the living as they postured and chatted. It was obvious from the way that they were grouped that the living were outnumbered by the dead these days. Outside, in the dim streets, he passed figures like tumbling decahedrons who bore their own fields with them as moved between realities. They were probably unaware of him as they drifted by, or perhaps saw him as some extra enhancement of whatever dream it was they were living. Flick, flick. Scheherazade's Baghdad. John Carter's Mars. It really didn't matter that you were still in Paris, although Elanore, of course, had showed sensitivity in the place she had selected for their meeting.

Beyond the last of the reality engines, Gustav's own cheap unvirtual tenement loomed into view. He picked his way across the tarmac towards the faint neon of the foreal Spar store beside it. Inside, there were the usual grey slabs of packaging with tiny windows promising every possible delight. He wandered up the aisles and activated the homely presence of the woman who served the dozen or so anachronistic places that were still scattered around Paris. She smiled at him—a living ghost, really; but then people seemed to prefer the illusion of the personal touch. Behind her, he noticed, was an antiquated cigarette machine. He ordered a packet of Disc Bleu, and palmed what were probably the last of his credits—which amounted to half a stick of charcoal or two squeezes-worth of Red Lake. It was a surprise to him, in fact, that he even had enough for these cigarettes.

Outside, ignoring the health warning that flashed briefly before his eyes, he lighted a Disc Bleu, put it to his lips and deeply inhaled. A few moments later, he was in a nauseous sweat, doubled up and gasping.

Another bleak morning, timeless and grey. This ceiling, these walls. And Elanore . . . Elanore was dead. Gone.

Gustav belched on the wine he was sure that he'd drunk, and smelled the sickness and the smoke of that foreal Disc Bleu still clinging to him. But there was no trace of Elanore. Not a copper strand of hair on his shoulder or curled around his cock, not her scent riming his hands.

He closed his eyes and tried to picture a woman in a white chemise bathing in a river's shallows, two bearded men talking animatedly in a grassy space beneath the trees and Elanore sitting naked close by, although she watches rather that joins in their conversation . . .

No. That wasn't it.

Somehow getting up, pissing cloudily into the appropriate receptacle, Gustav finally grunted in unsurprise when he noticed a virtual light flickering through the heaped and broken frames of his easels. Unlike the telephone, he was sure that the company had disconnected his terminal long ago. His head fizzing, his groin vaguely tumescent, some lost bit of the night nagging like a stray scrap of meat between his teeth, he gazed down into the spinning options that the screen offered.

It was Elanore's work, of course—or the ghost of entangled electrons that Elanore had become. Hey presto—Gustav was back on line; granted this shimmering link into the lands of the dead and the living. He saw that he even had positive credit, which explained why he'd been able to buy that packet of Disc Bleu. He'd have slammed his fist down into the thing if it would have done any good.

Instead, he scowled at his room, the huddled backs of the canvases, the drifts of discarded food and clothing, the heap of his bed, wondering if Elanore was watching him now, thrusting a spare few gigabytes into the sensors of some nano-insect that was hovering close beside him. Indeed, he half-expected the thin partitions and dangling wires, all the mocking rubbish of his life, to shudder and change into snowy Russian parkland, a wooded glade, even Paris again, 1890. But none of that happened.

The positive credit light still glowed enticingly within the terminal. In the almost certain knowledge that he would regret it, but quite unable to stop himself, Gustav scrolled through the pathways that led him to the little-frequented section dealing with artist's foreal requisites. Keeping it simple—down to fresh brushes, and Lefranc and Bourgeois's extra fine Flake White, Cadmium Yellow, Vermilion, Deep Madder, Cobalt Blue and Emerald Green—and still waiting as the cost all of that clocked up for the familiar credit-expired sign to arrive, he closed the screen.

The materials arrived far quicker than he'd expected, disgorging themselves into a service alcove in the far corner with a whoosh like the wind. The supplier had even remembered to include the fresh bottles of turpentine he'd forgotten to order—he still had plenty of clean stretched canvases anyway. So here (the feel of the fat new tubes, the beautiful, haunting names of the colors, the faint stirring sounds that the brushes made when he tried to lift them) was everything he might possibly need.

Gustav was an artist.

The hours did funny things when Gustav was painting—or even thinking about painting. They ran fast or slow, passed by on a fairy breeze, or thickened and grew huge as megaliths, then joined up and began to dance lumberingly around him, stamping on every sensibility and hope.

Taking fierce drags of his last Disc Bleu, clouding his tenement's already filmy air, Gustav finally gave up scribbling on his pad and casting side-long glances at the canvas as the blazing moon began to flood Paris with its own sickly version of evening. As he'd always known he'd probably end up doing, he then began to wander the dim edges of his room, tilting back and examining his old, unsold, and generally unfinished canvases. Especially in this light, and seen from upside down, the scenes of foreal Paris looked suitably wan. There was so little to them, in fact, such a thinness and lack of color, that they could easily be re-used. But here in the tangled shadows of the furthest corner, filled with colors that seemed to pour into the air like a perfume, lay his early attempts at Symbolism and Impressionism . . . Amid those, he noticed something paler again. In fact, unfinished—but from an era when, as far as he could recall, he'd finished everything. He risked lifting the canvas out, and gazed at the outlines, the dabs of paint, the layers of wash. He recognized it now. It had been his attempt at Manet's *Olympia*.

After Elanore had said her goodbyes to all her friends, she retreated into the white virtual corridors of a building near the Cimetière du Père Lachaise that might once have been called a hospital. There, as a final fail-safe, her mind was scanned and stored, the lineaments of her body were recorded. Gustav was the only person Elanore allowed to visit her during those last weeks; she was perhaps already too confused to understand what seeing her like this was doing to him. He'd sit amid the webs of sliver monitoring wires as she absently stroked Metzengerstein and the cat's eyes, now far greener and brighter than hers, regarded him. She didn't seem to want to fight this loss of self. That was probably the thing that hurt him most. Elanore, the proper foreal Elanore, had always been searching for the next river to cross, the next challenge; it was probably the one characteristic that they had shared. But now she accepted death, this loss of Elanore, with nothing but resignation. *This is the way it is for all us,* Gustav remembered her saying in one the last cogent periods before she forgot his name. *So many of our friends have passed on already. It's just a matter of joining them . . .*

Elanore never quite lost her beauty, but she became like a doll, a model of herself, and her eyes grew vacant as she sat silent or talked ramblingly. The freckles faded from her skin. Her mouth grew slack. She began to smell sour. There was no great fuss made when they finally turned her off, although Gustav still insisted that he be there. It was a relief, in fact, when Elanore's eyes finally closed and her heart stopped beating, when the hand he'd placed in his turned even more flaccid and cold. Metzengerstein gave Gustav one final glace before it twisted its ways between the wires, leapt off the bed and padded from the room, its tail raised. For a moment, Gustav considered grabbing the thing, slamming it down into a pulp of memory circuits and flesh and metal. But it had already been de-programmed. Metzengerstein was just a shell; a comforter for Elanore in her last dim days. He never saw the creature again.

Just as the living Elanore had promised, her ghost only returned to Gustav after a decent interval. And she made no assumptions about their future at that first meeting on the neutral ground of a shorefront restaurant in virtual Balbec. She clearly understood how difficult all this was for him. It had been a windy day, he remembered, and the tablecloths flapped, the napkins threatened to take off, the lapel of the cream brocade jacket she was wearing kept lying across her throat until she pinned it back with a brooch. She told him that she still loved him, and that she hoped they would be able to stay together. A few days later, in a room in the same hotel overlooking the same windy beach, Elanore and Gustav made love for the first time since she had died.

The illusion, Gustav had to admit, then and later, was always perfect. And, as the dying Elanore had pointed out, they both already knew many ghosts. There was Marcel for instance, and there was Jean, Gustav's own dealer and agent. It wasn't as if Elanore had even been left with any choice. In a virtual, ghostly daze himself, Gustav agreed that they should set up home together. They chose Brittany, because it was new to them—unloaded with memories—and the scenery was still often decent and visible enough to be worth painting.

Foreal was going out of style by then. For many years, the technologies of what was called reality had been flawless. But now, they became all-embracing. It was at about this time, Gustav supposed, although his memory once was again dim on this matter, that they set fire to the moon. The ever-bigger reality engines required huge amounts of power—and so it was that the robot ships set out, settled into orbit around the moon and began to spray the surface with antimatter, spreading their wings like hands held out to a fire to absorb and then transmit back to Earth the energies this iridescence gave. The power the moon now provided wasn't quite limitless, but it was near enough. With so much alternative joy and light available, the foreal world, much like a garden left untended, soon began to assume a look of neglect.

Ever-considerate to his needs, Elanore chose and had refurbished a gabled clifftop mansion near Locronan, and ordered graceful and foreal furniture at huge extra expense. For a month or so, until the powerlines and transformers of the reality engines had been installed, Gustav and Elanore could communicate with each other only by screen. He did his best of tell himself that being unable to touch her was a kind of tease, and kept his thoughts away from such questions as where exactly Elanore was when she wasn't with him, and if she truly imagined she was the seamless continuation of the living Elanore that she claimed herself to be.

The house smelled of salt and old stone, and then of wet plaster and new carpets, and soon began to look as charming and eccentric as anything Elanore had organized in her life. As for the cost of all this forgotten craftsmanship, which even in these generous times, was quite daunting, Elanore had discovered, like many of the ghosts who had gone before her, that her work—the dealing in stocks, ideas and raw megawatts in which she specialized—was suddenly much easier. She could flit across the world, make deals based on long-term calculations that no living person could ever hope to understand.

Often, in the early days when Elanore finally reached the reality of their clifftop house in Brittany, Gustav would find himself gazing at her, trying to catch her unawares, or, in the nights when they made love with an obsessive frequency and passion, he would study her whilst she was sleeping. If she seemed distracted, he put it down to some deal she was cooking, a new anti-matter trail across the Sea of Storms, perhaps, or a business meeting in Capetown. If she sighed and smiled in her dreams, he imagined her in the arms of some long-dead lover.

Of course, Elanore always denied such accusations. She even gave a good impression of being hurt. She was, she insisted, configured to ensure that she was always exactly where she appeared to be, except for brief times and in the gravest of emergencies. In the brain or on the net, human consciousness was a fragile thing—permanently in danger of dissolving. *I really* am *talking to you now, Gustav.* Otherwise, Elanore maintained, she would unravel, she would cease to be Elanore. As if, Gustav thought in generally silent rejoinder, she hadn't ceased to be Elanore already.

She'd changed, for a start. She was cooler, calmer, yet somehow more mercurial. The simple and everyday motions she made like combing her hair or stirring coffee began to look stiff and affected. Even her sexual preferences had changed. And passing over *was* different. Yes, she admitted that, even though she could feel the weight and presence of her own body just as she could feel his when he touched her. Once, as the desperation of their arguments increased, she even insisted in stabbing herself with a fork just so that he might finally understand that she felt pain. But for Gustav, Elanore wasn't like the many other ghosts he'd met and readily accepted. They weren't Elanore. He'd never loved and painted them.

Gustav soon found couldn't paint Elanore now, either. He tried from sketches and from memory; once or twice he got her to pose. But it didn't work. He couldn't quite loose himself enough to forget what she was. They even tried to complete that *Olympia*, although the memory was painful for both of them. She posed for him as Manet's model, who in truth she did look a little like; the same model who'd posed for that odd scene by the river, *Dejéuner sur l'Herbe*. Now, of course, the cat as well as the black maid had to be a projection, although they did their best to make everything else the same. But there was something lost and wan about painting as he tried to develop it. The nakedness of the woman on the canvas no longer gave off strength and knowledge and sexual assurance. She seemed pliant and helpless. Even the colors grew darker; it was like fighting something in a dream.

Elanore accepted Gustav's difficulties with what he sometimes found to be chillingly good grace. She was prepared to give him time. He could travel. She could develop new interests, burrow within the net as she'd always promised herself and live in some entirely different place.

Gustav began to take long walks away from the house, along remote clifftop paths and across empty beaches where he could be alone. The moon and the sun sometimes cast their silver ladders across the water. Soon, Gustav thought sourly, they'll be nowhere left to escape to. Or perhaps we will all pass on, and the gantries and the ugly virtual buildings that all look like the old Pompidou Center will cease to be necessary; but for the glimmering of a few electrons, the world will revert to the way it was before people came. We can even extinguish the moon.

He also started to spend more time in the few parts of their rambling house that, largely because much of the stuff they wanted was hand-built and took some time to order, Elanore hadn't yet had fitted out foreal. He interrogated the house's mainframe to discover the codes that would turn the reality engines off and on at will. In a room filled with tapestries, a long oak table, a vase of hydrangeas, pale curtains lifting slightly in the breeze, all it took was the correct gesture, a mere click of his fingers, and it would shudder and vanish to be replaced by nothing but walls of mildewed plaster, the faint tingling sensation that came from the receding powerfield. There, then gone. Only the foreal view at the window remained the same. And now, click, and it all came back again. Even the fucking vase. The fucking flowers.

Elanore sought him out that day. Gustav heard her footsteps on the stairs, and knew that she'd pretend be puzzled as to why he wasn't working in his studio.

"*There* you are," she said, appearing a little breathless after her climb up the stairs. "I was thinking—"

Finally scratching the itch that he realized had been tickling him for some time, Gustav clicked his fingers. Elanore—and the whole room, the table, the flowers, the tapestries—flickered off.

He waited—several beats, he really didn't know how long. The wind still blew in through the window. The powerfield hummed faintly, waiting for its next command. He clicked his fingers. Elanore and the room took shape again.

"I thought you'd probably override that," he said. "I imagined you'd given yourself a higher priority than the furniture."

"I could if I wished," she said. "I didn't think I'd need to do such a thing."

"No. I mean, you can just go somewhere else, can't you? Some other room in this house. Some other place. Some other continent . . . "

"I keep telling you. It isn't like that."

"I know. Consciousness is fragile."

"And we're really not that different, Gus. I'm made of random droplets held in a force field—but what are you? Think about it. You're made of atoms, which are just quantum flickers in the foam of space, particles that aren't even particles at all . . . "

Gustav stared at her. He was remembering—he couldn't help it—that they'd made love the previous night. Just two different kinds of ghost; entwined, joining—he supposed that that was what she was saying. And what about my cock, Elanore, and the stuff that gets emptied into you when we're fucking? What the hell do you do with that?

"Look, Gus, this isn't—"

"—And what do you dream at night, Elanore? What is it that you do you do when you pretend you're sleeping?"

She waved her arms in a furious gesture that Gustav almost recognized from the Elanore of old. "What the hell do you think I do, Gus? I *try* to

106

be human. You think it's easy, do you, hanging on like this? You think I enjoy watching *you* flicker in and out?—which is basically what it's like for me every time you step outside these fields? Sometimes I just wish I . . . "

Elanore trailed off there, glaring at him with emerald eyes. Go on, Gustav felt himself urging her. Say it, you phantom, shade, wraith, ghost. Say you wish you'd simply died. But instead, she made some internal command of her own, and blanked the room—vanished.

It was the start of the end of their relationship.

Many guests came to visit their house in the weeks after that, and Elanore and Gustav kept themselves busy in the company of the dead and the living. All the old crowd, all the old jokes. Gustav generally drank too much, and made his presence unwelcome with the female ghosts as he decided that once he'd fucked the nano-droplets in one configuration, he might as well try fucking them in another. What the hell was it, Gus wondered, that made the living so reluctant to give up the dead, and the dead to give up the living?

In the few hours that they did spend together and alone at that time, Elanore and Gustav made detailed plans to travel. The idea was that they (meaning Elanore, with all the credit she was accumulating) would commission a ship, a sailing ship, traditional in every respect apart from the fact that the sails would be huge power receptors driven directly by the moon, and the spars would be the frame of a reality engine. Together, they would get away from all of this, and sail across the foreal oceans, perhaps even as far as Tahiti. Admittedly, Gustav was intrigued by the idea of returning to the painter who by now seemed to be the initial wellspring of his creativity. He was certainly in a suitably grumpy and isolationist mood to head off, as the poverty-stricken and desperate Gauguin had once done, in search of inspiration in the South Seas; and ultimately to his death from the prolonged effects of syphilis. But they never actually discussed what Tahiti would be *like*. Of course, there would be no tourists there now— only eccentrics bothered to travel foreal these days. Gustav liked to think, in fact, that there would be none of the tall ugly buildings and the huge Coca-Cola signs that he'd once seen in an old photograph of Tahiti's main town of Papeete. There might—who knows?—not be any reality engines, even, squatting like spiders across the beaches and jungle. With the understandable way that the birth-rate was now declining, there would be just a few natives left, living as they had once lived before Cook and Bligh and all the rest—even Gauguin with his art and his myths and his syphilis—had ruined it for them. That was how Gustav wanted to leave Tahiti.

Winter came to their clifftop house. The guests departed. The wind raised white crests across the ocean. Gustav developed a habit, which Elanore pretended not to notice, of turning the heating down; as if he needed chill and discomfort to make the place seem real. Tahiti, that ship of theirs, remained an impossibly long way off. There were no final showdowns—just this gradual drifting apart. Gustav gave up trying to make love to Elanore just as he had given up trying to paint her. But they were friendly and cordial with each other. It seemed that neither of them wished to pollute the memory of something that had once been wonderful. Elanore was, Gustav knew, starting to become concerned about his failure to have his increasing signs of age treated, and his refusal to have a librarian; even his insistence on pursuing a career that seemed only to leave him depleted and damaged. But she never said anything.

They agreed to separate for a while. Elanore would head off to explore pure virtuality. Gustav would go back to foreal Paris and try to rediscover his art. And so, making promises they both knew they would never keep, Gustav and Elanore finally parted.

Gustav slid his unfinished *Olympia* back down amid the other canvases. He looked out of the window and saw from the glow coming up through the gaps in the houses that the big reality engines were humming. The evening, or whatever other time and era it was, was in full swing.

A vague idea forming in his head, Gustav pulled on his coat and headed out from his tenement. As we walked down through the misty, smoggy streets, it almost began to feel like inspiration. Such was his absorption that he didn't even bother to avoid the shining bubbles of the reality engines. Paris, at the end of the day, still being Paris, the realities he passed through mostly consisted of one or another sort of café, but there were set amid dazzling souks, dank Medieval alleys, yellow and seemingly watery places where swam strange creatures that he couldn't think to name. But his attention wasn't on it anyway.

The Musée D'Orsay was still kept in reasonably immaculate condition beside the faintly luminous and milky Seine. Outside and in, it was well-lit, and a trembling barrier kept in the air that was necessary to preserve its contents until the time came when they were fashionable again. Inside, it even *smelled* like an art gallery, and Gustav's footsteps echoed on the polished floors, and the robot janitors greeted him; in every way, and despite all the years since he'd last visited, the place was the same.

Gustav walked briskly past the statues and the bronze casts, past Ingres' big, dead canvases of supposedly voluptuous nudes. Then Moreau, early Degas, Corot, Millet . . . Gustav did his best to ignore them all. For the fact was that Gustav hated art galleries—he was still, at least, at painter in that respect. Even in the years when he'd gone deliberately to such places because he knew that they were good for his own development, he still liked to think of himself as a kind of burglar—get in, grab your ideas, get out again. Everything else, all the ahhs and the oohs, was for mere spectators . . .

He took the stairs to the upper floor. A cramp had worked its way beneath his diaphragm and his throat felt raw, but behind all of that there was this feeling, a tingling of power and magic and anger—a sense that perhaps . . .

Now that he was up amid the rooms and corridors of the great Impressionist works, he forced himself to slow down. The big gilt frames, the pompous marble, the names and dates of artists who had often died in anonymity, despair, disease, blindness, exile, near-starvation. Poor old Sisley's *Misty Morning.* Vincent Van Gogh in a self portrait formed from deep, sensuous, three-dimensional oils. Genuinely great art was, Gustav thought, pretty depressing for would-be great artists. If it hadn't been for the invisible fields that were protecting these paintings, he would have considered ripping the things off the walls, destroying them.

His feet led him back to the Manets, that woman gazing out at him from *Dejéuner sur l'Herbe*, and then again from *Olympia.* She wasn't beautiful, didn't even look much like Elanore . . . But that wasn't the point. He drifted on past the clamoring canvases, wondering if the world had ever been this bright, this new, this wondrously chaotic. Eventually, he found himself face to face with the surprisingly few Gauguins that the Musée D'Orsay possessed. Those bright slabs of color, those mournful Tahitian natives, which were often painted on raw sacking because it was all Gauguin could get his hands on in the hot stench of his tropical hut. He became wildly fashionable after his death, of course; the idea of destitution on a far away isle suddenly stuck everyone as romantic. But it was too late for Gauguin by then. And too late—as his hitherto worthless paintings were snapped up by Russians, Danes, Englishmen, Americans—for these stupid, habitually arrogant Parisians. Gauguin was often poor at dealing with his shapes, but he generally got away with it. And his sense of color was like no one else's. Gustav remembered vaguely now that there was a nude that Gauguin had painted as his own lopsided tribute to Manet's *Olympia*—had even pinned a photograph of it to the wall of his hut as he worked. But, like most of Gauguin's other really important paintings, it wasn't here at the Musée D'Orsay, this supposed epicenter of Impressionist and Symbolist art. Gustav shrugged and turned away. He hobbled slowly back down through the gallery.

Outside beneath the moonlight, amid the nanosmog and the buzzing of the powerfields, Gustav made his way once again through the realities. An English tea house circa 1930. A Guermantes salon. If they'd been foreal, he'd have sent the cups and the plates flying, bellowed in the self-satisfied faces of the dead and living. Then he stumbled into a scene he recognized from the Musée D'Orsay, one, in fact, that had once been as much a cultural icon as Madonna's tits or a Beatles tune. *Le Moulin de la Galette.* He was surprised and almost encouraged to see Renoir's Parisian figures in their Sunday-best clothing dancing under the trees in the dappled sunlight, or chatting at the surrounding benches and tables. He stood and watched, nearly smiling. Glancing down, saw that he was dressed appropriately in a rough woolen navy suit. He studied the figures, admiring they animation, the cleaver and, yes, convincing way that, through some trick of reality, they were composed . . . Then he realized that he recognized some of the faces, and that they had also recognized him. Before he could turn back, he was called to and beckoned over.

"Gustav," Marcel's ghost said, sliding an arm around him, smelling of male sweat and Pernod. "Grab a chair. Sit down. Long time no see, eh?"

Gustav shrugged and accepted the brimming tumbler of wine that offered. If it was foreal—which he doubted—this and a few more of the same might help him sleep tonight. "I thought you were in Venice," he said. "As the Doge."

Marcel shrugged. There were breadcrumbs on his mustache. "That was *ages* ago. Where have you been, Gustav?"

"Just around the corner, actually."

"Not still *painting* are you?"

Gustav allowed that question be lost in the music and the conversation's ebb and flow. He gulped his wine and looked around, expecting to see Elanore at any moment. So many of the others were here—it was almost like old times. There, even, was Francine dancing with a top-hatted man—so she clearly wasn't across the sky. Gustav decided to ask the girl in the striped dress who was nearest to him if she'd seen Elanore. He realized as he spoke to her that her face was familiar to him, but he somehow couldn't recollect her name—even whether she was living or a ghost. She shook her head, and asked the woman who stood leaning behind her. But she, also, hadn't seen Elanore; not, at least, since the times when Marcel's Venice when Francine was across the sky. From there, the question rippled out across the square. But no one, it seemed, knew what had happened to Elanore.

Gustav stood up and pushed between the twirling dancers beneath the lantern-strung trees. His skin tingled as he stepped out of the reality and the laughter and the music suddenly faded. Avoiding any other such encounters, he made his way back up the dim streets to his tenement.

There, back at home, the light from the setting moon was bright enough for him to make his way through the dim wreckage of his life without falling—and the terminal that Elanore ghost had reactivated still gave off a virtual glow. Swaying, breathless, Gustav paged down into his accounts, and saw the huge sum—the kind of figure that he associated with astronomy, with the distance of the moon from the Earth, the Earth from the sun—that now appeared there. Then, he passed back through the terminal's levels, and began to search for Elanore.

But Elanore wasn't there.

Gustav was painting. When he felt like this, he loved and hated the canvas in almost equal measures. The outside world, foreal or in reality, ceased to exist for him.

A woman, naked, languid, and with a dusky skin quite unlike Elanore's, is lying upon a couch, half-turned, her face cupped in her hand that lies upon the primrose pillow, her eyes gazing away from the onlooker at something far off. She seems beautiful but unerotic, vulnerable yet clearly available, and self-absorbed. Behind her—amid the twirls of bright yet gloomy decoration—lies a glimpse of stylized rocks under a strange sky, whilst two oddly disturbing figures are talking, and a dark bird perches on the lip of a balcony; perhaps a raven . . .

Although he detests plagiarism, and is working solely from memory, Gustav finds it hard to break away from Gauguin's nude on this canvas he is now painting. But he really isn't fighting that hard to do so, anyway. In this above all of Gauguin's great paintings, stripped of the crap and the despair and the self-justifying symbolism, Gauguin was simply *right*. So Gustav still keeps working, and the paint sometimes almost seems to want to obey him. He doesn't know or care at the moment what the thing will turn out like. If it's good, he might think of it as his tribute to Elanore; and if it isn't . . . Well, he knows that, once he's finished this painting he will start another one. Right now, that's all that matters.

Elanore was right, Gustav decides, when she once said that he was entirely selfish, would sacrifice everything—himself included—just so that he could continue to paint. She was eternally right and, in her own way, she too was always searching for the next challenge, the next river to cross. Of course, they should have made more of the time that they had together, but as Elanore's ghost admitted at that Van Gogh café when she finally came to say goodbye, nothing could ever quite be the same.

Gustav stepped back from his canvas and studied it, eyes half-closed at first just to get the shape, then with a more appraising gaze. Yes, he told himself, and reminded himself to tell himself again later when he began to feel sick and miserable about it, this is a true work. This is worthwhile.

Then, and although there is much that he still has to do and the oils are wet and he knows that he should rest the canvas, he swirls his brush in a blackish puddle of palette-mud and daubs the word NEVERMORE across the top and steps back again, wondering what next to paint.

First published in *Dying For It: More Erotic Tales of Unearthly Love*, edited by Gardner Dozois, 1997.

ABOUT THE AUTHOR

British writer **Ian R. MacLeod** was one of the hottest new writers of the nineties, and his work continues to grow in power and deepen in maturity as we move through the first decades of the new century. Much of his work has been gathered in four collections, *Voyages By Starlight, Breathmoss and Other Exhalations, Past Magic,* and *Journeys*. His first novel, *The Great Wheel,* was published in 1997. In 1999, he won the World Fantasy Award with his novella "The Summer Isles," and followed it up in 2000 by winning another World Fantasy Award for his novelette "The Chop Girl." In 2003, he published his first fantasy novel, and his most critically acclaimed book, *The Light Ages,* followed by a sequel, *The House of Storms* in 2005, and then by *Song of Time,* which won both the Arthur C. Clarke Award and the John W. Campbell Award in 2008. A novel version of *The Summer Isles* also appeared in 2005. His most recent books are a new novel, *Wake Up and Dream,* and a big retrospective collection, *Snodgrass and Other Illusions: The Best Short Stories of Ian R. MacLeod.* MacLeod lives with his family in the West Midlands of England.

The Issue of Gender in Genre Fiction: Conclusions

SUSAN E. CONNOLLY

What is the situation with women in SFWA-qualifying science fiction short story markets? What proportion of publications are authored by women? What proportion of submissions are authored by women? Is science fiction significantly different from the other genres in these markets? Can we see any trends that might explain the differences between markets?

These were the questions I wanted to ask when I began emailing editors back in the early months of 2014. In all honesty, I was not aware of the size or complexity of the task I was taking on when I began this study. As the data began to come in, and I saw the numbers of submissions that editors were categorizing for me, I gained an even greater appreciation for their assistance. This study has, in many ways, been a community project, with slush readers and editorial staff taking time out of their already busy working days to help provide valuable information to the science fiction and fantasy community.

Where We Are

Overall, authors who are women are less well represented in terms of submissions and publications than authors who are men. While some markets published more women than men in both all genres and in science fiction specifically, no market received more submissions from women than from men. However, markets displayed significant differences in terms of both submissions received, and stories published, for both science fiction alone, and all genres.

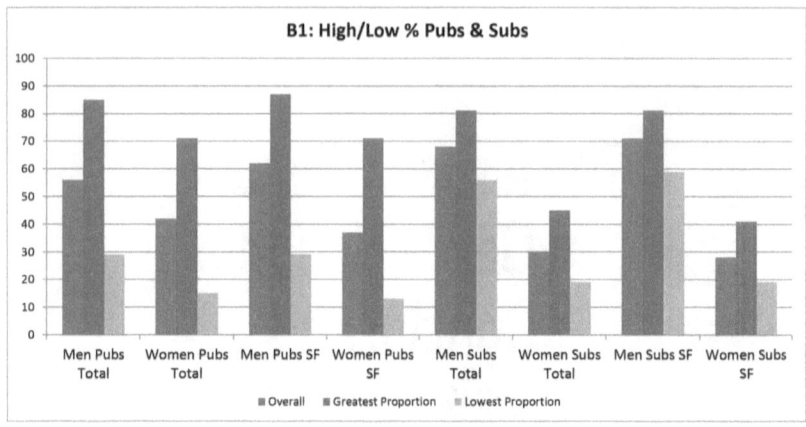

There are differences between markets, so there is something that *makes* a difference. What that is, we cannot say from our data. We found some relationships and correlations, but nothing we can point to and say, "This is it. If all markets made this change, we would see a greater representation of women authors."

Upon deeper analysis of multi-genre markets, I found that there was a correlation between a high proportion of women authors overall, and a high proportion of women authors of science fiction stories. However, we still found that women were, in many cases, not as well-represented in the science fiction section as they were in the market taken all together. Clearly, many of these markets are very friendly to authors who are women, and in some cases are attracting relatively high numbers of submissions by women, and still, science fiction is lagging behind other genres. The cause of this is unclear from our data, but it is an interesting result.

What Might Affect Gender Ratios?

Submissions

Age of senior editorial team, gender of senior editorial team, or whether a market is multi-genre or science fiction only had no relationship with the proportion of submissions received from women.

Publications

- Gender of senior editorial team had a moderate relationship with the proportion of published stories by authors who are men, but no relationship with science fiction stories.
- Age of senior editorial team had no impact on the proportion of women and men selected for publication.
- Science fiction only markets were more likely to publish stories by men than were the science fiction sections of mixed-genre markets.

Study Limitations: Submissions/Publications

Given the limitations of the data, it would be misleading to statistically analyze submission data and publication data together. The reasoning for this is given in the previous article, but in essence, it's because there are differing and inconsistent time lags between receipt of submissions and selection of stories for publication, and between acceptance of stories and the final publication date. We can't know from our data what the proportions of submissions were for a particular issue's publications.

No editor considered their submissions data to have an unusual proportion of men and women authors. A few points of percentage difference might not be noticed by an editor, but could lead to significant differences in statistical results. Hence, we can't really run correlative tests and so on for various factors. That said, we can draw general inferences from the submissions data, when considered with the publication data. Large swings of 10%+ would likely have been noticed by editors, so it seems fair to say that we can see large differences in the relative proportions of men and women selected from slush by different markets.

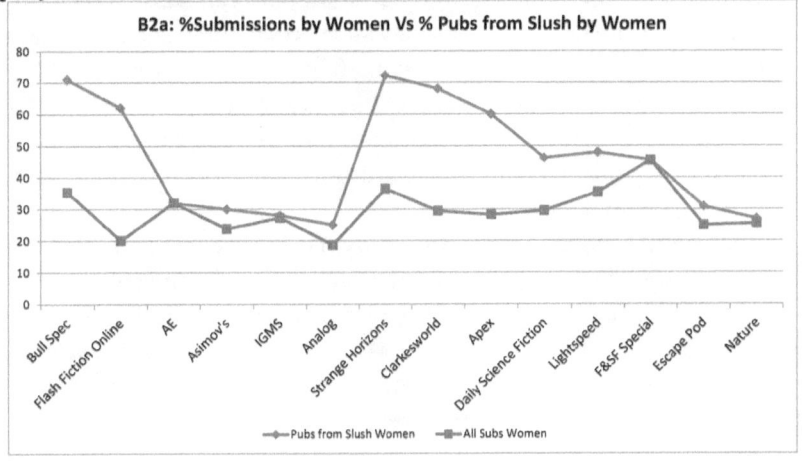

B2a: %Submissions by Women Vs % Pubs from Slush by Women

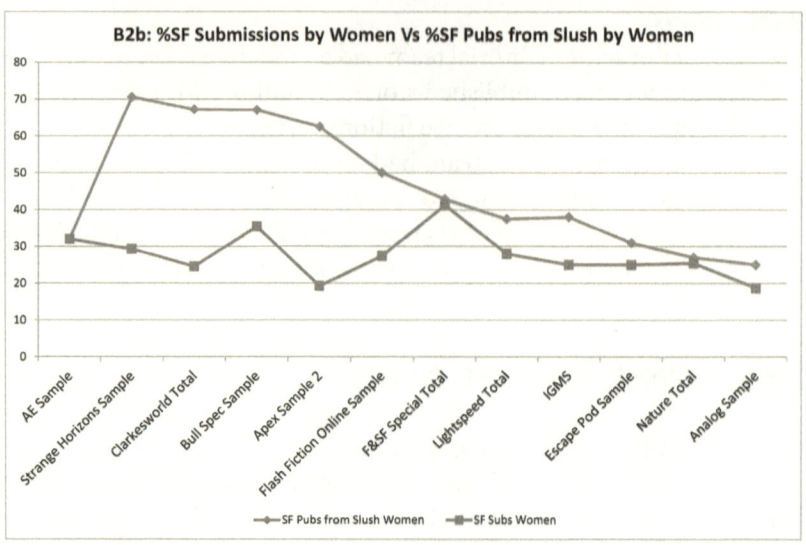

B2b: %SF Submissions by Women Vs %SF Pubs from Slush by Women

—◆— SF Pubs from Slush Women   —■— SF Subs Women

As you can see from the chart, it is not as simple an issue as saying, "We need to increase submissions by women," or "Markets who publish more women have greater numbers of submissions to choose from." While some markets closely track publications percentages to submissions percentages, other markets do not, showing that submissions ratios are not the only factor affecting publications ratios. Basically, we don't have an easy linear relationship between proportions of submissions by women and proportions of publications by women.

Whether or not increasing submissions from women would lead to an increase in acceptances from authors who are women is not a question I can answer from the data. I would need to compare markets over time, controlling for other factors that might affect acceptances. In addition, due to the time-lags and variation between submissions and publications, I can't run the tests necessary to say there is a statistically significant over-representation of women in publications, as compared to submissions. I can say that from a general reading, markets are at least matching their proportions of submissions, with some individual markets publishing a greater proportion of authors who are women than they have in submissions.

One useful outcome from this study has been a decision by some markets to update their guidelines to explicitly welcome submissions from authors who are women. Should this increase submissions from women, the time-study mentioned earlier would be possible, and the question of the relationship between submissions and publications ratios might be more easily answered.

At the start of June, *Escape Pod* made use of this strategy. In terms of raw numbers, their June submissions from authors who are women increased from an average of 19 of 75 total submissions (25% share), to 27 of 83 total, making up 32.53% of that month's submissions. July (up to the 29th of the month) showed a similar increase, with 36 submissions by women of 111 total, for a 32.43% share of submissions.

This is only a single market, and two months of data. However, apart from the updated guidelines and the announcements of such on Twitter, the only other changing factor, according to the staff, was an increase in pay to the new SFWA qualifying rate. While it is possible that this increase led to a greater number of submissions, it would not explain why women were more motivated by that increase than men. There is always the possibility that a third, more unlikely factor has caused this increase, but it does give an indication that such explicit welcoming of women may increase their share of submissions.

According to Nathaniel Lee of *Escape Pod*, their reasoning was simple. They discovered that they were receiving only a small proportion of submissions from women, and felt that the easiest-to-implement first step would simply be to encourage women to consider *Escape Pod* as a market. Whether this increase is a transient response or a sustained development is currently unclear, as is whether it will make an impact on the proportion of published stories by women. Even still, either result will give fruitful data for analysis and discussion.

Study Limitations: Gender Identification

One area in which this study was lacking was in data on non-binary individuals. In most cases, the gender categorization for each submission was based on first name, although some editors also engaged in Googling public bios of authors. As such, there are undoubtedly submissions from non-binary individuals which were miscategorized. Rose Lemberg raised this issue on Twitter, where it generated a fruitful discussion. Excitingly, a proposal was put forward suggesting that markets include an optional post-submission survey allowing for collection of demographic information based on the self-identity of authors. *Crossed Genres* expressed an interest in such a survey, and if there is follow through from markets, the full picture for both gender identity and other demographic areas would be much easier to analyze.

With that said the fact that we are looking at data on 'apparent' gender, does not invalidate the study. Rather, it gives us another factor to consider when we assess the rigor and implications of the results. I am grateful to all those who took part in the Twitter discussion for elaborating on these implications and effects.

Further Avenues for Study

My aim in carrying out this study was to answer some of the underlying questions about representation of men and women in science fiction. Discussion of this topic often reaches an impasse when differing contributors disagree on the potential causes of a problem or whether there is in fact a problem at all. I hope that at least some of these issues can now be more easily discussed, with common reference points for the actual circumstances.

However, to say that all the questions are answered is, of course, blatantly false. Firstly, there are the limitations of the data collection and analysis, which I hope have been made clear in all instalments of the study. Secondly, there is the fact that complete investigation of many of these questions would require different data, samples, and methodologies. Thirdly, there is the fact that there are important questions that I have not even attempted to answer.

During my communications with editors, a number of questions were raised which this data could not answer, but which would be fruitful areas for further research and discussion. Are women less likely to resubmit to a market after receiving a rejection? Are women less likely to submit the same story to a different market after it has been rejected elsewhere? Are women less likely to self-categorize a story as science fiction when submitting to multi-genre markets? Are women less likely to submit a story to a market that only publishes science fiction, perhaps due to this self-categorization issue?

I would very much welcome further research aimed at answering these questions. Post-submission surveys, along with the continued tracking of data which many publications have expressed an intention to carry out, will hopefully allow for follow-up and comparative studies. This data will hopefully better elucidate how various initiatives and strategies affect the submissions and publications gender ratios in the genre.

Overall, this study has been time-consuming, occasionally frustrating, and always challenging, yet has, I believe, revealed important data for the community. We have no smoking gun for the differing levels of women's submissions and publication rates across different markets. And yet, those differences do exist. This is an important realization. Again, I wish to thank all the editors and editorial staff who assisted, and the insightful comments from readers. The engagement and support of the community in investigating gender parity has been immense—we have not yet reached our destination, but our feet are firmly on the road.

ABOUT THE AUTHOR

Susan E. Connolly's short fiction and non-fiction have appeared in *Strange Horizons, Daily Science Fiction, The Center For Digital Ethics* and the fanzine *Journey Planet.* She is the author of *Damsel,* a middle-grade fantasy from Mercier Press and *Granuaile,* an upcoming historical comic book from Atomic Diner. Her degree in Veterinary Medicine given her strong opinions about the accurate portrayal of animal sidekicks in fiction. Susan lives in Ireland, near the mountains. Also near the sea. Also near the forest (Ireland is a small country).

Human Nature:
A Conversation with Peter Watts
JULIE NOVAKOVA

Deep sea, deep space, and deep dark corners of the human mind—these are some of the domains in which Peter Watts truly excels. His Hugo-nominated novel *Blindsight* opens with the main character trapped in a shuttle, reminiscing, escaping . . . from what? As we dive into the story, we encounter one question after another, all of them fascinating and urging us forward.

At the end, with his readers awe-struck and hungry, Watts leaves more questions than answers. Some of them might be addressed in his soon to be published novel *Echopraxia*, which is a sequel to *Blindsight*, but other, even more profound questions will without a doubt stem from the answers. Peter Watts is a master of thought experiments. That much was apparent even from his earliest short fiction in the nineties.

Being a marine biologist by study, Watts set his first novel *Starfish* three kilometers below the sea surface to a rift in the Juan de Fuca subduction zone. But in this deep-sea environment, something is different, and it's not only the strange outcast crew of Beebe Station. The success of *Starfish* was followed by publishing the two next books of the Rifters trilogy, *Maelstrom* and *Behemoth*.

However, Watts isn't at home just in the deep sea—deep space, be it the edge of the solar system in *Blindsight* or vastly distant stars like in the Hugo-winning novelette "The Island," is another environment he can depict so convincingly we can almost see the wonders of cosmos and the strange alien life forms before our own eyes. Watts's aliens have been often praised for being truly alien and at the same time very believable. His insight into an alien's mind in *The Things*, published here in 2010, led to another Hugo nomination. Peter Watts's fiction is full of brilliant ideas, the kind that urges us to ask: What if?

A friend of mine once commented about Watts: "He thinks of really interesting things."

It's a simple statement but also a very accurate one. Let me introduce you the man who thinks interesting things.

Your upcoming novel* Echopraxia *is a sequel to* Blindsight, *taking us inwards the Solar System to the Icarus Array this time. Have you already had an idea for this story when you were writing* Blindsight?

You know, I'm not entirely sure. It's natural, in the course of writing a novel, to mull over what might happen after the last page—so in that vague sense I was certainly thinking of a follow-up. At the same time, I knew that *Blindsight* would be a hell of a hard act to follow, whether or not it was any good in terms of literary merit. The thematic question of consciousness vs. intelligence is pretty fundamental to the human condition; what the hell do you do for an encore?

So while I was idly contemplating the idea of a sequel, the book I *really* expected to write after *Blindsight* was a near-future technothriller. It would have been a complete change of pace, and whether people loved it or hated it they'd be less inclined to compare it to *Blindsight* because it would have been so obviously a different creature. A straight-up sequel would, I thought, have a much harder time getting out from the shadow of its predecessor.

So what happened? I pitched about five different proposals to my agent, and he said the *Blindsight* sequel was head and shoulders above the others. And here we are.

Judging from the snippets you posted on your blog, *Echopraxia* seems to me that it won't have a hard time fulfilling high expectations.

Yeah, well, it's not as though I posted any of the crappy bits. Those snippets were probably high-graded.

Besides the prospects of meeting Siri Keeton's dad as one of the main characters and learning more about vampires and their role in the society, I was deeply intrigued by the Bicameral Order—a religious group whose predictions exceed those of science. Can you give us some hints about the methods they use, or their ideology and aims?

Hints. Hmmm.

The Dharmic faiths—you know, that school of thought that somehow, centuries ago, managed without benefit of MRI or TMS to figure out that all sensation, that the self itself, is an illusion—those Dharmic faiths were the mother of the modern Bicameral Order. (Neuroscience was the father; it was a winter-spring relationship.) But the Bicams aren't *really* a religious order in the conventional sense, except insofar as their origins trace back to those ancient faiths. Oh, and also in the sense that they undergo religious experiences—the so-called "rapture"—in the course of their work.

Then again, that whole transcendence/speaking-in-tongues thing happens when the part of the brain responsible for mapping body parts and boundaries fucks up. The mind loses its sense of where the body ends and the rest of the universe begins, so it literally ends up feeling connected to all of creation. The Bicams experience that because they're members of a hive mind. Sharing sensory systems, linking minds one to another—such connections really do dissolve the boundaries between bodies. So for them, religious rapture is an unavoidable side effect of networked existence.

Oh, and I guess they're also a religious order in the sense that they're faith-based—but faith has a very specific meaning here. There are certain sublevels of reality which are, even in principle, immune to empirical investigation. Anything below the Planck length gets very iffy; you can conjecture and model and hypothesize all you like, but as long as there's no way to test those conjectures you're not talking conventional science. (The various flavors of string and brane theory are regarded by many as philosophy, not science, for exactly that reason.) The Bicamerals have—at enormous personal cost, as it turns out—rewired themselves to explore reality past those limits, and the proof of their methodology is that they own half the patent office by the time *Echopraxia* opens. But it's not a *scientific* methodology. It can't be, by definition. We don't really have a word for what they do; but faith comes closest.

They're also a religious order in the sense that they believe in God. But that's not just faith: they have their reasons. Know your enemy and all that.

I guess maybe they're pretty religious after all.

You often explore topics related in many ways to religion in your works. When you mentioned the near-future technothriller, were you talking about your other upcoming project, Intelligent Design? Can you give away a little of what can we be looking forward to in this novel?

Well, yes, the title cuts two ways; I see the novel as both a straight-ahead Wattsian thought experiment (albeit hopefully more accessible than some of my previous efforts), and as a kind of metacommentary on the arguments of the IDiots who keep trying to sneak creationism into science classes. But in terms of what you can look forward to? You can look forward fifteen or twenty years to an ice-free Arctic, remote-controlled feral lobsters, genetically-engineered giant squid, submarine skirmishes between the US and Canada over wellheads on the Beaufort Shelf, and sentient money.

Assuming the damn thing even gets off the ground. And if "looking forward" is the right term.

Your novels tend to be elaborately structured in order to express innovatory ideas, especially Blindsight, where you modeled each of the central characters to reflect some part of consciousness. When you start writing a novel, do you have a highly detailed outline to which you try to stick or just a short synopsis, or do you use some different approach altogether?

That first thing—Cory Doctorow once said I didn't write outlines so much as "novels without dialog"—but it never works out. I usually get somewhere between halfway and three-quarters done before I realize that Plot Point C contradicts Plot Point G, or some new scientific discovery trashes some vital bit of narrative tech I've rested half the story on. At which point I pretty much have to throw away the outline and start flying by the seat of my pants, stitching up the seams in the crotch as they split.

Speaking of scientific discoveries requiring changing the story, you've repeatedly mentioned that you don't think that being a scientist is a good prerequisite for being a good science fiction writer. Since scientists are often trained by peer-reviewers' responses to use unnecessarily difficult writing in their papers, it often tends to make the work seem more complicated.

Yet, more scientists are trying to express their findings as simply as possible and even don't fear using humor (For example, I recently saw a sub-title: The good, the bad, and the ungulate). Do you think it's getting better or are these just exceptions?

My sense is, things are getting better. The use of personal pronouns, which was verboten back when I was going through grad school, is pretty common in the technical literature these days. It's not uncommon for research papers in journals to be chaperoned by relatively nontechnical summary articles aimed at the nonspecialist (though perhaps still not accessible to Josephine SixPack).

Hell, *Nature* regularly publishes science fiction. I can cite studies demonstrating a strong correlation between bafflegab and publication— one shows that the more opaque the writing style, the more prestigious the journal in which the paper ultimately appears—but those are all over a decade old by now. I don't know if their findings are still relevant.

In fact, the pendulum may be swinging too far in the other direction, what with scientists bending over backwards to "reach out" and "communicate with the masses." I hear this refrain with increasing frequency: it's *scientists* who are at least partly to blame for the public's skepticism over evolution and climate change and vaccination, because they don't try hard enough to communicate their findings to the general public. (Neil deGrasse Tyson is one of many who toe this line.)

I don't buy that. It's been pretty firmly established that Human Nature is so rife with Confirmation Biases and Backfire Effects that even if you present someone with ironclad, irrefutable, expert evidence that their cherished beliefs are wrong, they'll just dig in their heels and clutch those beliefs even closer to their bosoms (bosa? bosii?), while at the same time vilifying the expert who contradicted them. It's not that they don't understand the arguments; it's just that they'll reject anything that's inconsistent with their preferred worldview.

So what we seem to be getting is an increased dumbing-down of complex scientific issues to pander to people who read at a grade-three level. *Scientific American* turned into *Psychology Today* sometime when I wasn't looking. *Psychology Today* turned into the fucking *National Enquirer*. The internet slowly fills with *TED* talks rife with charismatic delivery and vacuous content. And people still don't give a shit about climate change.

That's one of the most discussed problems in science—should scientists try harder to educate the public, or is it a wasted effort? I personally hope it isn't though the evidence points elsewhere. Another problem—in fact, the one that drove you out of academic science in the mid-90s—is the politicization of science. Do you think the situation has in any way improved over time? After all, the policy of science publishing seems to be changing with more open-access publishing and demands for clear acknowledgment of any competing interests along with making used datasets accessible to everyone. Do you consider this a good trend?

If that is in fact the trend, then yes. I approve. I'll have to take your word on that score, though; I haven't been keeping close track since I left academia myself, so whenever the issue pokes through onto my radar it's generally in relation to some so-called "scandal" in which Republican ideologues demand endless transcripts and e-mails of political enemies in an attempt to stifle scientific research (the Virginia attorney general's harassment of Michael Mann is a particularly clear-cut example).

I don't consider that a particularly good trend.

Daniel Brüks, the protagonist of Echopraxia, is a scientist too; a field biologist, a living fossil in his time, if I may cite from the official synopsis. Do you think that field work will become redundant soon or will there be a use for it centuries from now?

Here's a couple of snippets from *Echopraxia* that address that:

> *Physics, officially. Cosmology. High-energy stuff. But it was all supposed to be theoretical; as far as Brüks knew the Bicameral Order didn't perform actual experiments. Of course, hardly anyone did, these days. It was machines that scanned the heavens, machines that probed the space between atoms, machines that asked the questions and designed the experiments*

to answer them. All that was left for mere meat, apparently, was navel-gazing: to sit in the desert and contemplate whatever answers those machines served up. Although most still preferred to call it analysis.

and

*"No, I mean, what were you even doing out in the field? There any species even left out there that haven't been RAMrodded and digitized?""The extinct ones," Brüks said shortly. Then, relenting: "Sure, you can virtualize anything in the lab. Still doesn't tell you what it's doing out in the wide wet world with a million unpredictable variables working on it."*We're already going down that road: for years now, mathematicians have been using automated "proof assistants" that presume to test and verify theorems—but we have to take their word for it, because apparently their automated analyses are opaque to human understanding. Science itself is becoming an act of faith.

That said, whether Brüks is right about the value of field work depends largely on how long it takes before Moore's Law lets us model those "million unpredictable variables" in electrons. I'll hazard no guesses as to how long that's likely to take.

Regarding predictions of future (though it's not the purpose of science fiction), many of your science fictional ideas had acquired their real-world analogs quite quickly ("head cheeses," outside metabolism, guilt-response-modulating drugs, deep-sea tourist cruises). Doesn't it sometimes almost scare you how fast are these things happening?

Oh yes. That's the problem with basing your fiction on cutting-edge research; it doesn't stay cutting-edge for long, and in my experience the stuff always fades in the rear-view mirror years before I would have expected it to. I suspect my books will stale-date pretty quickly.

This goes back to what you mentioned earlier, regarding my opinion that scientists don't necessarily make the best science fiction writers. I try, I really do—but it's a real effort to push beyond the current state-of-the-art. It's probably a vestigial reflex from my days as a scientist, when unwarranted speculation was frowned upon.

In another novel you're planning, Sunflowers, you venture into the very far future. It's set on the relativistic ship Eriophora, known to your readers from the Hugo-winning novelette, "The Island." The characters can literally watch the rest of the universe grow old, even though their own technology and culture stay essentially the same. How did you cope with presenting a universe far from now, seen through the eyes of characters similar to us?

Hell, that's the easy part—just steal the light show from the end of *2001: A Space Odyssey*. If the characters are similar to us, that's all they'd be able to comprehend when confronted with a truly transcendent future anyway.

But I didn't have to face that issue in "The Island;" the bioDyson entity that *Eriophora* encounters there was presumably a natural phenomenon, not some posthuman piece of magitech. We may not encounter it for another few billion years, but it could be quietly photosynthesizing away right now for all we know.

I also ducked that challenge in the two other stories I've written in the sequence so far, "Hotshot" (which appears in Jonathan Strahan's latest anthology *Reach for Infinity*), and "Giants" (which appears in an invisible book put out by Chaosium, although it may be appearing elsewhere soon since those bozos haven't paid any of their authors and are therefore in breach of contract, not to mention burying the release itself so virtually no one knows the fucking anthology even exists. But I digress.). "Hotshot" takes place this century, just before *Eriophora* sails, so the culture shock isn't so much of a challenge. "Giants" is another weird-phenomenon-outside-the-ship-tangly-domestic-discord-inside story.

I'm still working up the courage to confront what we've become after millions of years of cyclical rise-and-fall. I have the seeds of an idea: a small ship pops out of a freshly booted gate, a ship containing a single posthuman from one of humanity's immortality phases. She rides along with our crew and brings them some news from home—but rather than going into suspended animation between builds, she just wanders through the caverns and corridors of the ship for thousands of years while Sunday and her buddies sleep away the eons. Something profound happens to her during that time, but she refuses to talk about it afterward.

That's all I've got so far. But obviously, I'm going to have to grab this particular bull by the balls more than once before the cycle is finished.

Creating characters outside the scope of today's humanity is a challenging task; and as you mentioned in one older interview, many authors avoid showing the Singularity directly and rather go around it somehow. In my view, you're very good at making especially those characters who don't fit typicality and often are partially products of advanced technology. Was it difficult to write them, particularly Theseus's crew in Blindsight? *How hard do you have to imagine you're Siri Keeton?*

Ooooh.

Some of the more superficial aspects of my characters didn't take much work at all, since I Tuckerised real-world characters at least insofar as physical appearance and (roughly) profession went. Siri was more personal; I'm nowhere on the spectrum, and I like to think I have a vastly more refined set of social skills than our protag, but one or two of his more emotional moments do spring from autobiography.

I did know someone who was dying, and it took me forever to screw up the courage to reach out to him simply because I didn't know what to say (it turned out to be easier than I'd feared). I also had a tendency to shut down and go into what a former partner termed "battle-computer mode" when dealing with emotionally sticky issues; I'd see the tears rise in her eyes and feel nothing more than a sort of cold contempt that she'd resorted to such cheap emotional trickery so early in the game. (Or maybe that wasn't me so much as that particular relationship, which kinda sucked in a lot of ways. Certainly it's been years and years since I've felt the urge to boot up that mode.) Regardless; those were bits of Siri that came out of me.

You have to remember that I cheated when delineating that character, though. The story is told in first-person flashback, after Siri Keeton was traumatically rehumanised. The man in the narrative was repressed and shut down and in utter denial about who he really was; but the tale was told from the perspective of a much more self-aware Siri looking back on his earlier behavior. That let me humanize the telling, even during those parts of the tale when he wasn't especially human. It meant he wasn't really so alien after all.

ABOUT THE AUTHOR

Julie Novakova was born in 1991 in Prague, the Czech Republic. She works as a writer and an evolutionary biologist. So far, she has published three novels, some twenty short stories in Czech and one other story in English (*The Brass*

City in Penny Dread Tales Vol. Three: In Darkness Clockwork Shine). Her novels were *The Crime on The Poseidon City, Never Trust Anything* and *A Silent Planet.* Julie's short stories appeared in Czech speculative fiction magazines (*Ikarie, XB-1* and *Pevnost*) and anthologies. She's a severe were-workaholic (which means that most of the time she's quite lazy and she magically transforms the night before deadline).

Another Word:
Obstacles and Style
DANIEL ABRAHAM

My father is a songwriter and has been since before I was born. Many of the songs he writes take the form of stories with narrative arcs, characters, and resolutions at the end. One of the things he told me was that personal style—as a musician or a songwriter or a novelist—is made from all the ways you find to cover up your shortcomings.

I've come to like that idea a lot.

Imagine you pick up a book, open it at random and read:

> "Building a human was easy: the Auditors knew *exactly* how to move matter around. The trouble was that the result didn't do anything but lie there and, eventually, decompose. This was annoying, since clearly human beings, without any special training or education, seemed to be able to make working replicas quite easily."

If you're familiar with Terry Pratchett, it seems likely you'll recognize him, even if you haven't read *Thief of Time*. And that holds true for any writing by an author with a strong, distinctive voice. And part—I think most—of what creates that familiarity is the toolbox of shortcuts, habits, and challenges the author brings to the project.

There's a movie I watch every year or two by a director I hate. The director is Lars von Trier, and the movie is *The Five Obstructions*. It's a kind of documentary, which is part of why I like it better than anything else von Trier has done. In it, he finds a man who was a friend and mentor: Jørgen Leth. Leth had made once influential short film called *The Perfect Human*. Von Trier challenges him to remake the film five times, each time with a different set of constraints. So, for the first remake, von Trier insists that 1) the film be shot in Cuba, 2) no sets be employed, 3) all the rhetorical questions asked in the original film be answered, and 4) that no piece of film be longer than 12 frames long (about half a second). Leth's response was to make a version of his work that was, to my tastes, more interesting and engaging than the original.

Four more times—or maybe only three, depending on how you count the last one—the original film is recreated with new constraints and limitations. Each one is fascinating in its own way, and watching a brilliant, creative man pushed to his limits is—for me, at least—better than sports. Each time the rules get harder in new ways. Sometimes Leth despairs. But then there is a moment where he smiles and starts to get excited. He's found his way around the problem, and his solution becomes the thing that makes that particular version interesting.

In the last few years, I've been lucky enough to be involved with several examples of a story being remade in a new medium. I adapted George R.R. Martin's, *A Game of Thrones* as a series of graphic novels, and I helped to adapt my own co-written novel *Leviathan Wakes* into a television show that will be airing next year. In both cases, the strengths of the novel matched poorly to the needs of the new form. Like Leth remaking *The Perfect Human* under different constraints, we had to retell the old story in a new way. Where the books had exposition, the graphic novels had visual imagery. Where the books had internal monologue and unreliable narrators, the TV show has the impartial eye of the camera. By changing the conditions under which we could tell the story, we changed the experience of it. It became something that was clearly related, but different.

You can see something like it when the world changes things around a genre too. Police procedural and suspense novels in the 1990s struggled to revamp the standard plots to fit a world of ubiquitous cell phones and Internet access. Sometimes they were successful, other times . . . well, less so. One novel I particularly remember made a point of using an ampersand in a domain name. But over time and with experience, writers learned ways to include new technologies into the plots, and even exploit new opportunities for suspense that hadn't been possible before. The style of plotting changed because the world played the role of von Trier to our communal Leth. *Tell the same story again, but the characters can always update each other instantly no matter how far apart they are.*

These examples of adaptation and remaking are important because they throw a light on the relationship between obstacles and creativity.

They let us see the same project done under different conditions. But sometimes limitations *don't* change. Sometimes—maybe often, maybe always—there are constraints that never go away.

The best poetry reading I ever went to was by a friend and former professor of mine who stuttered. I knew that was the case because I knew him, but the ways he'd found to incorporate the idiosyncrasies of his body into the delivery of his poems worked beautifully. And, because the other poets at that same reading weren't dealing with that issue, they didn't sound like him. He stood out.

I remember seeing a dance recital by a man on crutches and recognizing the way he'd incorporated his particular body into the movements. But the truth is, if it hadn't been for the cue of the crutches, I wouldn't have attributed his style to anything in particular other than his own identity as a dancer. I've seen other performers whose works were probably shaped by other things—a tricky knee or a particularly long waist or an old injury that healed poorly—that I couldn't recognize the origins of. I've heard poets read without knowing that they tended to avoid certain words or rhythms that they had a hard time pronouncing. I've seen paintings discussed as satire or social commentary or explorations of material that might have suddenly become much more explicable in a context of mental illness or the paints and dyes available to people in abject poverty.

If there were a single, objective standard for excellence—and I don't believe there is, but if—then those who excelled would also converge. The best writers would be the ones who adhered to the rules most closely: who never used passive voice, who always showed and never told, who didn't include any unnecessary words. They would be the same voice, and so they'd be voiceless. Thankfully, the world doesn't work like that.

We are our bodies, and we are our minds, and we are even (to some degree) our circumstances. None of us work quite according to spec. We're all flawed, and the best artists among us find ways to pause the way Jørgen Leth did, smile, and incorporate the work-arounds into what we do. So do the best non-artists. And everyone, really.

Whether our styles are pleasing or challenging or annoying, whether we're writing or dancing or working in an office, our strengths and talents make us competent. Our flaws and failings—and the ways we've invented to work despite them—make us interesting.

God save us from one without the other.

ABOUT THE AUTHOR ────────────────────────────────────

Daniel Abraham is a writer of genre fiction with a dozen books in print and over thirty published short stories. His work has been nominated for the Nebula, World Fantasy, and Hugo Awards and has been awarded the International Horror Guild Award. He also writes as MLN Hanover and (with Ty Franck) as James S. A. Corey. He lives in the American Southwest.

Editor's Desk:
Having an Adventure with Dad
NEIL CLARKE

This month, my father and I will embark on a little adventure. In a few days, we'll pack up our bags and board a flight bound for Dublin, Ireland. We'll be spending most of our time in Navan, the town in which my parents were born and grew up. My parents visited "home" just a few years ago, but it's been almost thirty years since I've been back. Most of my aunts, uncles, and cousins are still in Ireland. In the time I've been gone, some of my cousins have had children and became grandparents. I've lost count of just how many of them there are, but I look forward to seeing everyone again. It's been too long.

I'm particularly looking forward to doing all this with Dad. I recall my childhood trips to Ireland quite fondly and remember him dragging us around, showing my brother and me the castle he used to play in, the school where the Jesuits used to beat the children, and all manner of other events. The difference this time is that I'm old enough to appreciate it and smart enough to write some of it down. It will be his time to show off and it will be followed by mine.

After Ireland, we're heading to London for Worldcon. He isn't planning on attending, but I'm taking him anywhere I can. That Sunday is my birthday and I'm celebrating by bringing him to the Hugo Awards events with me: the reception for nominees, the ceremony, and the Hugo Loser's Party. I've never had a member of my family at one of these ceremonies, so win or lose, I'll be happy because he's with me. As a child, he once told me that if there was ever a book I wanted, he'd buy it for me. I think it's time he experiences the consequences of that action. I can only hope that my actions inspire my own children similarly someday.

If you'll be at Worldcon, maybe I'll see you there. Otherwise enjoy the rest of your summer!

ABOUT THE AUTHOR

Neil Clarke is the editor of *Clarkesworld Magazine,* owner of Wyrm Publishing and a current Hugo Award Nominee for Best Editor (short form). He currently lives in NJ with his wife and two children.

About the Artist

JULIE DILLON

Julie Dillon is a science fiction and fantasy illustrator creating art for books and magazines, as well as for her own projects and publications. She has won two Chesley awards, and has been nominated for two Hugo Awards and two World Fantasy Awards.

WEBSITE

juliedillonart.com